RIVER MAGIC

THE ELEMENTAL KEYS BOOK 1

LYNNE CANTWELL

hearth/myth

TABLE OF CONTENTS

Chapter 1 – Sunday

I've always loved the water. Which is what put me in the perfect position to find that drowned kayaker in the first place.

It was predestined, in a way. Although "inherited" works, too. My mother also loves water; she said she named me Raney because it tasted like rain.

She also said she knew as soon as she conceived that I would be a girl. I've never been impressed by that. I mean, she had a fifty-fifty chance of being right.

Anyway, Mam made sure we always lived near a body of water, even if it was only a swimming pool. A drainage ditch wouldn't do; the water needed to be deep enough for us to immerse ourselves in. She always took me with her until I hit my teens and didn't want any of the kids at school to see me hanging out with my mother.

Anyway, the point is that living near water was traditional for our family. It was a must, really, and a tradition I have happily carried on. Well, that's not strictly true – happiness doesn't have anything to do with it. I just kept doing it without thinking about it. You know how you grow up thinking everybody does the stuff your family does, and then you go to some other kid's house and realize how weird your family actually is?

But I can't *not* do it. Live near water, I mean.

The kayaker. Right.

This was a few years ago. I was taking a mid-career break by disappearing for a while to hike the Appalachian Trail. I'd moved to California to try to break into acting. But the movie business is so phony – it's all about appearances, and I'm not into that. I mean, I know I'm cute, but beautiful requires an absurdly early makeup call, and glamorous is just not happening.

Regardless, I'd had some success – I'd landed the lead of a moderately successful crime drama – but we'd been doing it for a few seasons by this point and honestly, the scripts were starting to sound derivative. Plus I'd just broken up with a handsome but arrogant jerk who thought the smartest thing I could do for my career was to capitalize on what I truly was.

It wasn't so much that I cared about the secret getting out, although I did. But I couldn't let anyone do that to Mam. I'd taken precautions to protect her – I used a fake last name, Meadows, professionally, even though my legal last name is the same as Mam's.

Anyway, after I kicked the ex out, I needed some time away from Hollywood to clear my head. So I left for a while. And that's why I was hiking the A.T. along the Shenandoah River near Harpers Ferry, West Virginia, that Sunday morning in August. It was hot and sticky, and the river looked inviting – so inviting that I struck off along a game trail to get closer to the water.

There, stuck in a tangle of broken branches near the bank, I spotted something neon green. I edged closer, and realized it was a technical hoodie – the kind watersports enthusiasts wear. Moreover, someone *was* wearing this one.

I shucked my pack and my boots and waded into the murk.

I didn't have to get very close to know the guy was dead. His blond ponytail, floating free of the flotsam he was stuck in, was the only lively thing about him. He wore jeans, which seemed at odds with his hoodie – I would have expected board shorts, or maybe a wetsuit.

Although if he were a thrill-seeker, it didn't make much sense for him to be here. The Shenandoah didn't have the kind of white water that attracts adrenaline junkies. Those guys tended to aim for the class IV and V rapids downriver on the Potomac in Great Falls National Park, or so my guidebook said. But the Shenandoah could get up to class III on a good day. And I'd heard the last time I'd stopped in a town that the river was running higher than usual, thanks to the remnants of a hurricane that had dumped several inches of rain on the mountains as it passed through to the upper Midwest.

Maybe this guy only *wanted* to be a thrill-seeker. Or maybe he bought the jacket because he liked it. In any case, I didn't need to rescue him. With a regretful look at the victim, I waded back to shore, fished my cell phone out of my pack, and called 911, grateful for the signal and a decent charge on the phone. Then I put my boots back on and hiked up the incline to the trailhead near the road, careful to skirt piles of deer scat on the way. The dispatcher had asked me to wait for the cops, so they wouldn't have to waste time looking for the body.

The first to arrive was a female cop, which shouldn't have surprised me as much as it did. "Officer Hartley," she said, offering a hand to shake.

"I'm Regina Heath," I said, which would work until somebody recognized me – which I thought unlikely, given that I'd been wearing the same sweaty clothes for three days.

"You found the body?"

I nodded. "I spotted his jacket first. You can't miss it – it's bright green." I grinned briefly. "The guy seems to be caught in some debris along the bank."

"You didn't go in after him, did you?" she said with a frown.

"Of course I did," I said. "What if he were still alive?"

She didn't answer. Instead, she said, "The county dive team is on their way. I need to stay up here and direct traffic. Stick around, would you? You'll need to show the team where the body is."

"Sure," I said, sighing inwardly. I'd hoped to put a lot more miles behind me today, but it looked like I'd be stopping over in Harpers Ferry.

Another police cruiser pulled up, and a spare, graying man with a mustache unfolded himself from the driver's seat. "Chief Craig Coburn," he said as he approached me. "Are you the hiker who found the body?"

I nodded, and repeated the conversation I'd just had with Officer Hartley. While we stood there talking, the dive team showed up. I was grateful to cut the conversation short and lead them down the trail.

One of the team members called over his shoulder, "You think we've found our floater, Chief?"

"Maybe," Chief Coburn said. "You tell me."

"Floater?" I asked another member of the team.

"We had an empty kayak fetch up along the bank downriver from here a few days ago," he explained. "This could be the missing guy."

"Ah," I said. I didn't know what else to say, so I led the way silently down the steep bank.

When we reached the river, I glanced back and saw someone with an impressive-looking camera tailing us. I stepped away from the bank and let the dive team get to work. Then I joined the photographer.

"Allen Owings from the *Harpers Ferry Sentinel*," he said by way of greeting. "Are you the hiker who found the body? Can I ask you some questions?"

"Sure," I said. He pulled out his phone and pointed the mic at me, and I went through it all again. Then he excused himself to get photos of the recovery operation. I didn't have anything better to do, so I stuck around to watch.

A few moments later, Chief Coburn descended the bank to supervise the team in the water. Allen Owings descended on him, and I moved closer to eavesdrop.

Owings pulled out his phone again and pointed it toward the police chief. "What's going on here, sir?" he asked.

Coburn sighed, then assumed the air of a professional cop. "The department received a report about an hour ago from a through-hiker about a bright green object in the water." He nodded toward me. "That's her, over there."

"I've already spoken with her," Owings said, not looking at me. "What happened then?"

"Well, we sent an officer out to investigate. She determined the object in the water was a body and called for the dive team. We're in the process of recovering the body now."

"Any idea who it might be?"

He shook his head.

"Description of the victim?" Owings pressed.

"All we know is he was a white male, long blond hair in a ponytail, wearing a green jacket and blue jeans."

Owings frowned. "No wetsuit? So he's not our missing kayaker."

"That's speculation. I can't confirm that."

"Sure. Of course not." Owings paused for a moment. "Have you checked with our local outfitters about any missing customers?"

"We're working on that. But what I can tell you for sure is we've received no reports of anyone missing from any sort of watercraft within the past forty-eight hours," he said.

"What about missing persons reports?" Owings asked.

"No," he said, and seemed about to say more, but we heard a shout from the river. "Excuse me," Coburn said, and loped off down the trail. Owings and I traded a look. Then he followed the chief, and I followed him.

The divers had succeeded in cutting the body free. I saw a flash of neon green as they slid the guy into the body bag. Then they carried him up the trail to the waiting ambulance.

As I said, I have an affinity for water. As the divers passed me with the bag, my mouth fell open in surprise. I couldn't help myself – I followed the divers up the trail and stood there, dumbfounded, while they loaded up the ambulance and it pulled away. No flashing lights, no sirens – no need to hurry with this guy. Nope, he had a date with the county medical examiner to confirm his cause of death, presumably by drowning.

Except he didn't drown. That's what had startled me. As soon as the divers had walked past me with the body, I knew the victim had no water in his lungs. I didn't know what had killed him, but it wasn't trying to breathe water. Of that much, I was sure.

Officer Hartley gave me a lift into town and some suggestions for a place to spend the night. "We have several hotels on the bypass," she said.

"Sounds good," I said. "Any with a soaking tub?"

She laughed. "Sore from all that hiking, huh?"

"Something like that."

She tapped her finger on her chin. "Let me call a friend of mine. She has an Airbnb that might be available." She glanced over at me. "She rents it for longer stays, too. You might want to think about that. I'm sure the chief will want to talk to you again."

"Swell," I said. I didn't have to be back in L.A. by any certain date, although I knew our producer was getting antsy. But the longer I stayed somewhere, the more likely it was that someone would recognize me – and I really didn't want to have to deal with a swarm of publicity hounds. I had a lot of trail left to hike, and I didn't want to be responsible for any paparazzi risking their lives by trying to follow me without proper camping gear. Not to mention clogging up the A.T. for other through-hikers.

By the time we made the short drive into town, Officer Cindy Hartley and I were on a first-name basis. She called her friend with the Airbnb and confirmed it was available. She handed over her cell phone and I gave the owner my credit card info for the deposit. Then my new best friend Cindy dropped me at the house.

It wasn't until I shut the door to my new digs and began mulling over the day's events in the silent apartment that it occurred to me it could have been a murder.

That was a fairly shocking thought. I knew from my pre-hike research that Harpers Ferry was a tiny town at the confluence of the Shenandoah and Potomac rivers. It was best known for the raid by abolitionist John Brown on the U.S. arsenal in 1869, prior to the start of the Civil War. That song we all learned in elementary school — *The Battle Hymn of the Republic?* "John Brown's body lies a-moldering in the grave"? That's the guy.

After Brown was hanged, the area had been the site of several Civil War battles, thanks to its strategic location for river traffic. But things had been pretty quiet since then. The town subsisted on tourism dollars from Civil War buffs who came to visit the Harpers Ferry National Historical Park and A.T. through-hikers like me. These days, a lot of residents commuted to jobs in D.C. every weekday. Cindy Hartley had told me there were only four officers on the whole police force, including Chief Coburn and her. Most of the crimes they had to contend with were vandalism-related. Even accidental deaths were rare.

Who would have killed the guy? Why here? And why dump his body in the river?

Then I started to get weepy. A man had met an untimely end — a man whose body I had been *thisclose* to physically.

My affinity for water made me a soft touch for the weak and downtrodden — for anyone who suffered. My ability to *feel* emotions deeply was crazy useful to me as an actor, but sometimes it annoyed the hell out of me.

There was a guy dead who shouldn't have been. The unfairness of it all threatened to overwhelm me.

I couldn't stay here right now. I needed water — big water — to disperse the big feelings I was having. Cursing my soft-hearted self, I unhooked the daypack from my behemoth pack and went out.

For a while, I walked aimlessly, trusting in my innate ability to find the precise stretch of water that would do me the most good. When I took stock of my surroundings again, I realized I was very near the scene of the crime — or, at least, the place where the body had been found. Well, if healing was to be had, I supposed, it made sense that I'd find it here. I blew my nose on a ratty tissue I found in the bottom of the daypack, sneezed from the dust accumulated on the ratty tissue, blew my nose a second time, and headed down the main trail.

I scuffed along, wondering why I hadn't left my jacket in my room. The humidity had popped up along with the temperature, and I was beginning to sweat.

When I got down to the water, I was a little surprised to find that the cops had strung crime scene tape all over the place. I guessed they thought they might need to come back for a more thorough investigation.

In any case, it didn't affect my plans. I sat on the bank downstream from the snag of debris that had caught the floater, pulled off my shoes and socks, and dabbled my feet in the water. As I watched them dissolve and re-form, over and over again, I succumbed to my emotions and began to sob.

My tears ceased abruptly when I realized I wasn't alone.

A short distance in front of me, a face formed in the river. It hovered just below the surface. It had long, green hair that seemed to want to stream away with the current, but the face stayed in the same spot, the eyes watching me. Pleading with me.

I took off my jacket and the rest of my clothes, put them next to my shoes on the riverbank, and slid into the water.

I should have skipped the wading and done that to start with. My corporeal body became one with the river, each droplet of me dancing with a droplet of the river water. Cleansing me of the pain and sorrow I'd felt at the man's passing. Releasing me from its grip.

This was what Mam had taught me when I was just a child: "Our kind," she had said as we soaked one day, "need this release. When the world of men has become too much for us, we need cleansing."

"But I'm not like you," I'd protested, my words all bubbly. "Not really."

"My dearest child, you're like me in all the ways that count," she said, adding sadly, "except you have a soul."

"What does that mean, Mam?" I'd asked. I didn't know anything about souls then. But she hadn't replied.

Now that I was older, I knew why it was so important to her that I have a soul. She'd risked everything to make sure I had one, and I appreciated her sacrifice. Loved her for it, even. But part of me still wished I hadn't had to be half-mortal to get one.

My vain regret, too, washed away. I was half-undine, half-mortal, and that was all there was to it.

As I began to pull myself together, the face reappeared before me. As wrapped up in healing as I was, I'd nearly forgotten why I'd dived into the water in the first place. "Hail, river goddess," I said politely, as I dissolved again. "Thank you for reminding me of the needs of my kind. In what manner should I address you?"

"I am Shenandoah," said the goddess, her voice deep and rolling. "You are welcome for the reminder, child of Water. But that is not why I welcome you to my domain."

"Oh?"

"The human your police officers found here today..."

The droplets that were me quivered, but not from the current. "Yes. And I know you were not responsible. He was murdered."

"I know. His mortal body bled into my waters as his life ebbed away. It was not...natural."

Murder typically isn't. I didn't say that to the river, though. It didn't seem like the sort of humor she would appreciate. And anyway, she seemed distraught. "I am sorry you had to go through that," I said instead.

"Now I must purify myself of this tainted blood," she said.

"I am sorry," I repeated.

"But that is not why I called you here."

I faltered. "You called me?"

The face materialized before me again. "I made sure you would come here. I made sure the body stuck fast here, in this place. I knew it would draw you."

"You knew…" I stopped in disbelief. The tiff with my ex-boyfriend, my decision to escape L.A. and hike the A.T. on a whim – all of it had led me to this moment, here, now?

I had a million questions, but the one that came out was, "Why me?"

"You are known to us."

"I…" Now I was really at a loss. "How? Why?" *And who's us?*

"Your mother is known to us."

"I don't understand any of this," I said. "You keep saying 'us'. And what does my mother have to do with anything?"

The face bowed slightly. "I do not communicate this way very often. I apologize for being cryptic. Potomac joins me in this."

That made sense. The two rivers flowed together at Harpers Ferry; it stood to reason the Potomac's deity would have skin in the game, too. "And my mother?"

"The Undine sent us a current that you were near."

If I'd been corporeal at that moment, I would have rolled my eyes. Mam always did have a tendency to be a helicopter parent – or whatever the watery equivalent of a helicopter would be. A submarine, maybe. "Thank you for looking after me," I bubbled, attempting to keep the snark out of my tone.

"You misunderstand," Shenandoah rumbled. "We are not your guardians. You are *our* guardian. And we need your help."

Could a Water Elemental be considered a guardian of rivers? It didn't seem to be the time for a philosophical discussion, so I set the question aside to think about later. "What can I help you with? I am only half-undine, as you know."

"You are undine enough for this," she assured me. "And in any case, you are the only one nearby. Hearken to me, Undine! With this murder, the normal order has been upset. We beseech you to help us right the wrong that has been done."

"I don't know how to filter blood from you," I said doubtfully.

"That is not what we need from you," she said. "I am not making myself clear. This murder — it goes against the normal order. It is wrong. That wrong must be righted."

"By me?" I squeaked. "But I'm not a cop..."

"Other forces are at work," Shenandoah intoned. "An ancient being has awakened. Ancient animosities have once again come into play. Order must be restored."

"And you think I'm the woman to do it?" I said. "I don't..."

"You must!" she roared, her voice like a cataract. "You are our only hope!"

Ancient words of a different kind seemed to echo from the banks. *Help me, Obi-Wan...*

"This is crazy!" I said. "I'm no superhero."

"Then all is lost." Her mournful rasp sounded like the barest trickle of moisture in a desert creek bed. "This land, the waters, the Two-Leggeds and the Four-Leggeds, the Plant People and the Rock People — everything. All will be lost if you will not help."

Water creatures love melodrama. Water equals emotion and all that stuff. Still, her despair, no matter how overwrought, tugged at my heartstrings. I sighed to myself. "All right. I still don't think I'm the right person for the job. But I'll do what I can."

The river goddess bowed again. Then her eyes flicked to the bank. "Someone comes," she said, and shimmered away to nothing.

CHAPTER 2 – STILL SUNDAY

Belatedly, I recalled that I'd left my clothing on the bank. I debated whether to stay put, but decided it would be better to get out and get dressed. Who knew how long the person would stay? And what if it were the cops coming back? They'd bag up my clothing and consider me a missing person and…

I lifted myself from the water, reassembling as I went – and froze halfway up. Someone wasn't coming – he was already here.

"Uh," he said.

Cheeks burning in embarrassment, I snatched up my shirt to cover my breasts, and tried pulling myself the rest of the way out one-armed. It worked about as well as you'd think. "Turn around!" I yelled.

"Oh. Yeah." He whirled and presented is back to me. "Sorry," he mumbled.

"Thanks." I sat on the bank and pulled on my bra and the rest of my clothing, then combed my hair back from my face as best I could. Mam was the sort of graceful creature who bobbed up from the deep with her hair all slicked back neatly, but I'd never mastered the art. "Okay," I said as I reached for my socks. "You can turn around now."

I saw him glance first, to make sure the coast was absolutely clear. Then he faced me. "Where did you come from?" he asked. "It was like you materialized or something."

"Or something," I said, getting to my feet. I hooked my jacket with a finger of my left hand and draped it over my shoulder.

"I'm Collum Barth." As we shook hands, I sized him up: short, although not stunted, and stocky, with square fingers, blunt at the tips. His brown hair hung even with the collar of his flannel shirt and his full, curly beard obscured the slogan on his black t-shirt. He wore a green cap – one of those droopy things that were all the rage when knitting was hot a few years ago. "And you are...?"

"Regina Heath," I said, but he was too busy squinting at me to pay attention.

"You look so familiar..." Then his mouth dropped open. "Wait a minute. You're Raney Meadows!"

Oh, great. He's seen my tits and *he's a fan.* "That's me," I admitted.

"You're so great in *Story of a Homicide,*" he went on. "I had trouble remembering you weren't a cop. Tough as nails."

"Thanks," I said. "That's the idea."

He ignored that, too. "This is a real stroke of luck," he said, relief in his eyes. "Maybe you can help me."

What is it with the world needing my help today? "I don't know...Collum, is it?" When he nodded, I said, "What do you need help with?"

His face kind of crumpled. "My brother's been missing for several days. I've been trying to find him, but he just isn't anywhere. And then today, I tracked him here."

Tracked seemed oddly significant, but I put that aside for the time being. Instead I said, "Your brother doesn't have a bright green hoodie by any chance, does he?"

"Yeah, he does. Why?" When I didn't answer right away, he said, "He's dead, isn't he?"

"Yeah," I said. "Yeah, he is."

He was quiet for a moment, staring at the ground between us, his mouth working behind the beard.

"I'm sorry," I said, not knowing what else to say. He nodded, still staring silently at the earth. The silence stretched. Five seconds. Ten.

If he stayed quiet for much longer, I was going to start to puddle up again. "Let me buy you a beer," I said. He nodded and followed me up the slope.

There was no vehicle parked along the road at the trailhead. "Where's your car?" I asked.

He stared at me as if I were speaking another language. "I walked."

From where? was on the tip of my tongue – we were pretty much surrounded by forested hills – but I stopped myself from asking. The guy had just lost his brother. It wouldn't be fair to pry. Instead, I stifled a sigh and hooked a thumb toward town.

For a moment, his eyes gleamed. "I know a shortcut," he said, and struck off into the woods on a trail I hadn't noticed before.

"Is the Private Ensign okay?" he said as we walked. "It's an Irish pub just off the historic area."

"Sure," I said. "You're the tour guide. I just got here."

He stopped and regarded me with a serious look. "Listen, Ms. Meadows," he began.

"It's Raney. Please."

He dipped his head in acknowledgement. "Raney." Then he stared at the dirt for a moment.

I had a feeling I knew where this was going, but he was having trouble articulating it. So I helped him. "You weren't surprised to hear your brother was dead," I observed.

His head came up abruptly. He gave me a small, relieved smile, then sobered. "I wasn't."

"And you're thinking maybe it wasn't accidental," I went on.

He looked at the dirt again and shook his head. "It wasn't."

"And you want me to help you find his killer." *Because I do it all the time on TV.*

He gave me almost the same hopeful look as Shenandoah had a few minutes before. But he said, "You don't have to do this."

I knew that. And I knew I was probably the least qualified person he could have asked for help. But it occurred to me that helping him might dovetail with helping the river goddesses. I flashed him a smile and said, "But I'm gonna."

He settled back into step with me. "Well, thanks." And that was it for conversation until we got to the pub.

The Private Ensign looked to be pretty popular with the locals. A sign by the door advertised live music on Friday and Saturday nights, and on Tuesdays amateurs with an interest in Irish music were invited to bring their instruments and commandeer the place. I was familiar with the idea of a session, as it was called. Sometimes the locals played better than the paid acts.

Today, however, it was relatively quiet. We flashed our IDs at the bouncer at the door — an African-American guy, the first I'd seen since getting to town — and went in to find seats. As we wended our way through the mostly empty tables, I felt eyes on me. I turned and saw the bouncer staring at me. He nodded — not in recognition, it seemed, but in approval. Feeling unsettled, I followed Collum to a table in the far corner.

Once we'd ordered — Guinness for him, a local I.P.A. for me — I leaned forward and said, "Sorry again about your brother. And I'm sorry to have sprung the news on you the way I did."

He sighed. "It's okay. I knew something bad had happened when he wasn't at his house."

"So you don't live together?"

"Oh, heck, no. Conor has no interest in living in the hills. After he graduated from college, he got himself a little house here in town." He sniffed. "When I went by to check on him, his cat was all over me." He chuckled bitterly. "That cat has never liked me. But she sure loved on me when I was there yesterday. I know how to fill her food bowl, you see."

"I see." I waited for a moment. "Were there any other signs…?"

"Oh, yeah. Conor's mail had piled up. He's got one of those old-fashioned slots in the front door, and there was a ton of stuff on the floor behind the door."

"He still gets mail?" I said, surprised. "Nobody ever sends me anything."

"Well, you know. Ad circulars and catalogs. That kind of junk." He paused. "I guess I need to tell all his magazines and things to stop sending him stuff." He rubbed his eyes with one hand and sniffed.

Just then, the waitress delivered our drinks. Collum chugged about a third of his and wiped his mouth on the sleeve of his flannel shirt. "It always tastes better in Ireland," he said, with an obvious effort to change the subject. "I don't know why."

"I've heard that. So you've been to Ireland?" I took a smaller swig of my beer.

"A few times. We have family there." He sighed. "Guess I'll have to contact them, too." He stared into his glass for a moment, then took another long swallow.

"What did Conor do for a living?" I asked.

"He's a geologist," Collum said. "He was working on a project for Alex Drake."

"Am I supposed to know who Alex Drake is?"

He shot me a rueful look. "Probably not. He's our state representative." He took another gulp of beer. "He's the perfect politician – tall, dark-haired, handsome, and without a brain in his head. He may run for Congress – and if he does, he'll probably win."

"He's that popular?"

"More like he knows people with lots of money," he said. "And they like him. A lot."

"Sounds like a bad combination for the little guy," I said. "What was your brother working on for him?"

"Some kind of big development on one of the islands in the river. Conor was over for supper last weekend and he was talking about it. He said Mr. Drake was paying him big money to do this analysis, but Conor could tell right off that it wasn't going to work."

"Why's that?"

"Well, those islands out there are nothing but rocks, really. The area's unstable – the river shifts all the time, and of course it's prone to flooding in the spring. And then, too, he'd have to get the Park Service to approve it."

That got my attention. "This Alex Drake is trying to develop Park Service property?"

"That's what my brother said." He took another swig of Guinness and made a face. "It's not as good when it's warm. Anyway, Conor said he had a meeting with Mr. Drake on Thursday. Planned to deliver the bad news then. That's the last time I saw him." He glanced up at me and away.

"Did you hear from him at all after that?"

He looked at me again. "No."

I counted on my fingers. Yeah, a cat would get pretty hungry after three days without food.

Collum drained his glass and placed it carefully on the table. "Thanks for the beer. I gotta go." His mouth twisted under the beard. "I need to pick up that damn cat and take it home with me."

"You should call the police," I said. "Tell them you're Conor's next of kin. They'll be able to tell you what to do now." I studiously avoided using the word *autopsy*.

"I guess I should," he said. Then he turned to me earnestly. "Would you do something for me, though?"

"Sure," I said.

"Would you look into this thing Conor was working on? See if you can find out anything? It might be tied to…"

I held up my hand. "I'm not actually a cop, you know," I said. "I only play one on TV. I know I said I'd help you, but this is starting to sound dangerous. You should probably let the real police handle it."

His eyes met mine. "I'd feel better if it was you."

"Why?"

"I just have a feeling about it, is all." He looked away again.

I let the silence stretch for a few seconds. Then I said, "Tell me something. When we were down by the river, you said you'd tracked your brother there."

"Yeah." He looked sideways at me.

"How?"

17

"What do you mean, how?"

I put my hands on the table and leaned forward. "All right. This is between you and me, okay?" I waited for him to nod before going on. "I'm pretty sure your brother didn't die where he was found. In fact, I'm very sure of it. Never mind how. But he was killed elsewhere and his body was thrown in the river. It got caught in that pile of debris along the bank there."

He sucked in a breath and nodded.

"So how could you track him? His feet never touched the ground there. What were you tracking?"

"How did you come together out of nothing when you came up out of the river?" he shot back.

I sat back. "It's complicated," I said.

"I'll bet."

We eyed each other warily for a few moments. Then he stood. "Let me know what you find out," he said.

"How do I get in touch with you?" I asked.

"I'll find you," he said, and walked out.

I had no doubt that he could.

The bouncer watched him go, and then turned to me. His eyes seemed to bore into me. His pupils were enormous. I felt like I might fall into them – and not in a good way.

Thoroughly weirded out, I chugged the last of my beer and dashed past the guy, out into the street.

There was no sign of Collum Barth – but then I didn't really expect there to be. I was beginning to wonder if I'd dreamed the whole thing, starting with Shenandoah's face in the river.

CHAPTER 3 – MONDAY, AND THEN TUESDAY

I spent Monday changing the plans for the remainder of my trip. I had no idea how long the police in Harpers Ferry wanted me to stick around, but I figured I'd plan for a week off the trail. So I pulled out my map, and canceled and rebooked motel reservations in towns farther along the route. Then I found the closest grocery store and laid in a stock of food for the next several days. I also had a long soak in the tub and decided it was acceptable.

Early Tuesday morning, I got a text from Cindy Hartley. The county medical examiner was planning to give a press conference that day, in case I wanted to be there.

Of course I wanted to be there. I'd promised Collum that I'd look into his brother's death. But moreover, I wanted to hear what the M.E. had to say about how the man had died.

A little before the appointed time, I arrived at the police station with a notebook and pen. I figured if I looked like a reporter, they might let me stay. The receptionist pointed me in the direction of the conference room but the door was closed, so I camped out on the floor outside and pretended to write something in the notebook.

Fifteen minutes later, a TV crew – a sweet, young thing who had to be the reporter, and her videographer – showed up. They opened the door to the conference room and went in to set up their equipment. I shrugged to myself, pulled my stuff together and followed them in. "Hi," I said to the sweet, young thing. "Regina Heath."

"Oh, hi," she said, smiling brightly. "Julie Andrews, WDVM in Hagerstown. Hi, Steele!" She waved at another camera crew coming in the door. I recognized the reporter, Steele Moser, from seeing him on TV the night before. His mane of white hair was hard to miss.

Steele glanced our way, gave a cursory wave, and huddled with his videographer.

More news people trickled in: Allen Owings, the photographer I'd met at the scene on Sunday; and a reporter wearing a dorky name badge that proclaimed he worked for a paper in Winchester. Everybody seemed to know everyone else, except for a woman who placed a recorder on the podium and took a seat next to it.

I sidled over to where Allen was sitting. "Who's she?" I asked.

"Frida somebody. She's with the AP," he said. He did a double-take. "What are you doing here, anyway?"

"I got invited," I said.

"By who?"

I raised my finger to my lips as a side door opened and Chief Coburn entered the room. He was followed by another man who I figured was the M.E.

Chief Coburn approached the podium, which was now bristling with microphones. "Thank you all for coming," he said without preamble. "As you know, on Sunday afternoon our department, with the aid of the Jefferson County sheriff's office dive team, retrieved a body from the Shenandoah River. We have identified the body as that of thirty-five-year-old Conor Barth of Bolivar. Previous to the recovery of his body, Mr. Barth had been missing for several days."

I nodded to myself. *Collum must have taken my advice and contacted the police.*

The next moment, though, I wasn't so sure. "Mr. Barth's employer, Hookbill Incorporated, had not heard from him since the prior Monday," Coburn went on. "His employer has positively identified the body for us. We've been told he had no next-of-kin. Now I'll turn you over to Dr. Edwin Munsing, Jefferson County medical examiner, for his findings."

I frowned. Conor's *employer* ID'd the body? That seemed highly irregular to me. And why did Hookbill Inc. tell the cops that he had no next of kin? Why hadn't anybody tried to find Collum?

I shelved my questions and turned my attention to Dr. Munsing.

"Thank you, Chief Coburn." The doctor cleared his throat and stared fixedly at his notes on the podium before him; clearly, he wasn't used to any sort of limelight. "Ladies and gentlemen. I conducted a preliminary autopsy on the body of Mr. Conor Barth yesterday morning. We are still awaiting the toxicology report, which will take another several weeks. But my initial findings are consistent with drowning as the cause of death."

I gasped. I couldn't help it. Heads turned in my direction.

Munsing looked up. "Questions?" he said hurriedly. He looked like he wanted to flee.

"Dr. Munsing, I have a question," the AP reporter said. "When you say your findings are consistent with drowning, what led you to that conclusion?"

"I found no visible marks on the body," he said, "and a sufficient quantity of water in his lungs to have caused his death."

Bullshit.

"And do you have any idea how long he'd been dead?" she asked.

"As I said, my findings are preliminary. But given the state of the body when it was recovered, I would place his time of death at five to seven days prior."

Bullshit again. Collum had dinner with him three days ago. I half-listened as the other reporters lobbed a few questions at the good doctor. Then Coburn released him from purgatory and took the podium again.

"As you may know," he said, "a kayak was found abandoned last week in Great Falls National Park. Pending the results of the toxicology report, we believe Mr. Barth is our missing kayaker, and we are ruling his death as accidental."

21

I knew Conor hadn't drowned. Why had the M.E. lied? Had someone pumped water into Conor after the divers picked him up? If so, why? And who killed him?

"Any more questions?" Coburn asked.

I spoke up. "Chief Coburn, have you tried to locate any of Mr. Barth's relatives?"

He eyed me warily. "No," was all he said. Then, "If there are no more questions, thank you for coming." And he ushered Dr. Munsing out the side door.

Allen Owings paused in the act of flipping his notebook shut and eyed me with interest. "You sure seemed startled by the cause of death. What do you know that I don't know?"

I weighed my answer for a moment. "Let's just say I have a lot more questions now than I did when I walked in. Nice to see you again." And I left before he could ask me anything else.

After lunch, I stopped by the library to use their free wi-fi. I wasn't exactly a whiz at research, but I figured it shouldn't be too hard to check out Collum's story. After all, if Conor had been working on a development project for Alex Drake, there ought to be something filed officially – either with the town of Harpers Ferry or with Jefferson County or both.

Or neither. My Google-fu turned up no projects that fit the description Collum had given me.

I did hit pay dirt, of a sort, on Conor's employer. The cops hadn't made up Hookbill Inc. It was an engineering firm located in Shepardstown, up the Potomac from Harpers Ferry. Their website featured a few projects the company had been involved in – roads and bridges, systems for controlling water runoff, that sort of thing. I didn't see anything about ongoing projects, but I did learn that engineering firms usually work with other construction companies – which maybe I should have known, but I'd never had any reason to think about it before. Anyway, the owner or general contractor might have filed for the permit with the county, which could explain why I hadn't found one under Mr. Drake's company's name.

Except I also hadn't found anything on a project like the one Collum had described to me. And if the company was far enough along in the planning to have hired engineers, *somebody* at the county level ought to know about it.

On a whim, I burrowed into local real estate sales records. Again, I turned up nothing.

Maybe I *had* hallucinated everything: the conversation with Shenandoah, having a beer with Collum, and that bouncer with the weird eyes.

Except Collum had given me his brother's name, and it was the same one the cops had.

I googled Conor and got his address in Bolivar, the little town adjacent to Harpers Ferry. I'd gotten the impression that people who wanted to be near the commuter train to D.C. but who didn't want to live in a historic district, with all the zoning restrictions that entailed, often lived in Bolivar instead.

I looked at the clock on the library computer and realized I'd run out of free wi-fi. Time to head home.

As I headed back to my apartment, I toyed with the idea of walking past Conor's place – not to go in, but just to size it up, talk to the neighbors, and see if the cops had actually been there. I was still suspicious about how they were taking his employer's word for who he was and how long he'd been gone. But my feet seemed to move of their own accord – toward the Private Ensign.

I mean, I needed to eat anyway. I could probably use a beer, too – I was still pretty keyed up from the press conference earlier in the day. And it was session night. At least there'd be music.

I remembered reading somewhere, while preparing for my hike, that Harpers Ferry, like the rest of the Appalachian Mountains, was settled by people originally from England. But Irish laborers came in the 1800s to help build the Chesapeake and Ohio Canal and they brought their music with them. Making music wasn't among my talents, but I appreciated the emotional journeys music could take me on.

It was early when I got to the bar, but some musicians were already there to grab the best seats near the fireplace. Tables had been pushed back to make room for a tiny dance floor, in case anyone was moved to do a jig. I ordered shepherd's pie and a pint of beer and relaxed, intending to let go of my troubles for the evening and live in the moment.

The musicians began trickling in, greeting one another as they began tuning up. One was a fellow with a shock of red hair who played the fiddle as if the devil himself were after him. Another was a woman who played the tin whistle; her style was sweet, but not as showy as the fiddler's. It was her clothing that made her stand out. She wore a top with billowy sleeves that seemed to sway in time with the music.

I'd say the crowd numbered about twenty-five folks, all told, with ten of them musicians – another fiddler, a guitarist, a woman with an accordion, several people with tin whistles, and a fellow with a drum called a bodhran whose hand moved so fast when he played that his mallet was a blur. Nobody led the group. Someone would call out the name of a tune and they'd all join in, playing one song after another. I clapped and cheered and ordered another pint.

Then as the musicians struck up another tune, a man got up from the audience and went to the dance floor. He was short and stocky and wore a green knit cap, and he began to dance – no, he began to caper. This wasn't a Riverdance performance – he leapt and twirled like an Irish dervish, if such a thing existed. By the end of the song, the musicians cheered as loudly for him as I did. He bowed low – and then as the players struck up a reel, he walked to my table and held out a hand to me.

"Oh, no," I said, my hands held up in front of me.

"Oh, yes," he said, grabbing my hands and pulling me to my feet.

"I don't know what I'm doing!" I cried.

"Just follow me," he said. "It's easy." And he began to move his feet – slowly at first, so I could follow along. It didn't take me long to catch on, maybe because Collum held my hand the whole time. It almost felt like he was transferring some of his dancing talent to me through touch.

So things were going pretty well – until the musicians stepped up the pace.

I tried to keep up, but it was useless. Laughing, I kind of shifted from one foot to another while Collum finished the set with a flourish of hops and kicks that Michael Flatley himself would have envied. Another round of wild applause, and I led the madman back to my table, calling for a Guinness for him and another beer for me.

"You remembered," he said with an engaging grin. He wiped his brow with the cuff of his flannel shirt.

"I remembered you?"

"No, you remembered that I drink Guinness."

"It seems an integral part of your character, now that I've seen you dance."

He accepted his pint from our waitress and began to drink in one continuous motion, waggling his eyebrows at me over the rim of his glass. I raised my glass to him with a laugh and took a drink myself. Dancing was thirsty work, even for one as lousy at it as I was.

He set down his glass and nodded toward the fireplace. "We're about to have company," he said. Sure enough, two of the musicians – the crazed fiddler and the diaphanously-sleeved whistle player – had their heads together and were gesturing toward us. They rose and, leaving their instruments behind, approached our table.

"We have a bet," the fiddler said, "and you're the only one who can settle it."

"Go on," said Collum.

"We'd like to know whether you're pure leprechaun or only half."

Collum threw back his head and laughed. "You'll get no pot of gold from me either way." He gestured expansively. "Join us."

"We'd love to," said the whistle player, and they pulled chairs over while Collum signaled the waitress to bring us another round.

"Do you all know one another?" I asked.

The musicians exchanged a glance. "We've only just introduced ourselves to each other tonight," the whistle player confessed. "I'm Gail Oleander." She looked toward the fiddler.

"Rufus MacKay," he said. "And you, my mysterious friend?"

"Collum Barth." Before I could stop him, he hooked a thumb at me and said, "And this is Raney Meadows." He leaned in. "*The* Raney Meadows."

I rolled my eyes at him. "Nice to meet you all," I said.

"Your name seems so familiar," said Gail to me.

Collum leaned forward and said, as if imparting a state secret, "She's on TV." Then he drained his glass.

"Drowning your sorrows, Collum?" asked Rufus.

Collum's smile vanished. His gaze dropped to the table as he said, "Yeah, actually. My brother just died."

The usual round of *I'm so sorry* followed. I admit I was grateful – I didn't want to talk about my job just then.

No luck, though. "How did he die?" Gail asked.

In answer, Collum looked at me.

I sucked in a breath. "The police say he drowned."

"Drowned? Is this the…?" Gail looked from Collum to me, and then back to Collum again. "Oh, no. Oh, that's terrible."

Collum shrugged and drank deeply of his new glass.

Rufus raised an eyebrow in my direction. "You sound as if you don't believe them."

"Yeah. It's complicated. But I don't."

"Why would they lie?" Rufus asked.

I raised my glass to him. "An excellent question. I wish I knew the answer."

"Well, how do you *think* he died?" Rufus pressed.

The only excuse I have is that I'd had a couple of beers and things were getting a little hazy around the edges. "Well, he didn't drown. I know that for sure. He had no water in his lungs."

"And how do you know that?" Collum said.

"That's not what they said on the news," said Gail at the same time.

I chose to answer her. "I know that's not what they said. I was at the press conference when the M.E. announced his findings." I looked at Collum. "But the M.E. lied. I was there when the cops pulled your brother from the river."

"I know," he said. "That's why I came to find you."

"That's what I thought," I said. I very nearly put voice to the thing I never say to anyone – the thing that sets me apart from humanity – because I was certain his secret was much the same as mine.

But he turned from me to the others and the spell was broken. "I've asked Raney to help me find out who killed Conor."

I looked at Rufus and Gail. "Conor worked for an engineering firm called Hookbill Incorporated," I said. "Have either of you heard of it? I couldn't find out much information about them online."

Rufus sat back with a slow smile. "Oh, yeah, I've heard of them. They're the reason I'm here. I've spent the past six months trying to organize their workers."

"Organize…?" I said. "You're with a union?"

"Laborers' Union International," he said. Belatedly, I noticed the *Union – Yes!* pin he wore on his lapel. "We've had lots of complaints from their workers about how unfairly they're treated. They're like slave labor." His complexion darkened as he spoke. "Of course, the company would like to keep doing business as usual, so they're not too happy to have us around, talking to their employees. There's been some trouble."

"Really?" I said.

"What about this project on Virginius Island?" Collum asked.

"Virginius?" asked Gail. "That's National Park Service property."

27

"Right," said Collum. "That's the project my brother was working on. Some kind of big development, he said."

"Why would anyone want to develop Virginius Island?" Gail asked. "The place always floods. There hasn't been anything there since the 1930s."

"I don't know why," Collum said. "But Raney's going to help me find out."

"I spent some time looking today, but there's nothing on file with the town planning commission," I said.

"It would have to be approved by the Park Service," Gail mused. "I'm a volunteer docent for the park. It's sort of my job since I retired from the government a few years ago. I'll ask around."

"Thanks," Collum said.

"So Collum," Gail said, "what do you do for a living?"

"Oh, this and that," he said. He nodded toward the fireplace where the musicians were reassembling. "I think you're going to be needed over there shortly."

"Right," said Rufus. "Thanks for the drink. Oh, Raney – here's my card." He fished his wallet out of his back pocket and handed me a business card. "Call me. I'd love to tell you about what's going on at Hookbill."

"I'll call you later this week," I said with a smile, and slid his card into my purse.

Collum watched this interplay a little too closely. I decided it was time to derail his train of thought. "So what *do* you do?" I asked him as our new friends went back to their original seats. "Or should I be asking, what do you guard?"

His nostrils flared as he realized what I was asking him. "If I tell you," he said, "I'll need to know which river is your home."

I smiled archly. "It's not a river."

"What is it, then?"

"I asked you first."

28

He smiled — and in the space between one heartbeat and the next, we were no longer in the Private Ensign. Instead, we were outdoors in the fading sunlight, standing before the gate of an odd little cabin. Its shape blended into its surroundings in ways Frank Lloyd Wright had only dreamed of — the walls were the same color as the surrounding foliage and the roof line followed the curve of the ancient mountain ridge above.

"So I was right," I said. "You're a gnome." An Earth Elemental.

"Half right," he admitted. "My father is a gnome. He built all this." He gestured at the house. "My mother was human." He cocked his head. "And you're an undine."

"You're half right," I said. "Mam's the full undine. I never knew my father — she took me back to the water when I was small."

"I knew it," he breathed. With the slightest nod, he opened the gate. "Please come in. We have so much to talk about."

I hesitated. "What about paying for our drinks? And my dinner?"

"I run a tab," he said. "I'll square it with them tomorrow." He took my hand. "Come on. There's nothing to be afraid of."

CHAPTER 4 – STILL TUESDAY, HERE AND THERE

While we're here on Collum's threshold, I should probably explain more about how this whole Elemental thing works.

Today, thanks to science, we know that humans are made mostly of star stuff. Well, and water. We're something like ninety-eight percent water. Which is why, when a person is cremated, the resulting ash only fills a small box.

But philosophers and early scientists thought there were four Elemental building blocks, if you will, that created everything on earth. Those Elements were Earth, Air, Fire, and Water. And it wasn't just Western civilization that came up with that list. Native American nations assigned these Elements to the cardinal directions of their medicine wheels, and they'd never even heard of Paracelsus.

Who's Paracelsus, you ask? I was just about to tell you. He was the Swiss philosopher who, during the Renaissance, sort of codified this Elemental system. He also named a fifth Element, Aether, which is basically a void – the space between the other Elements or the space where they hung out. Something like that.

Anyway, the other thing Paracelsus did was to suggest that certain magical creatures represented or embodied the Elements. For Water, it's undines. For Earth, it's gnomes. For Air, it's sylphs. And for Fire, it's salamanders – but magical salamanders, not the kind you'd find in your backyard. Fire salamanders can both create fire and survive it.

Over the centuries, we've also had certain qualities attached to us. For example, Water corresponds to emotion; as I said, I feel things deeply and I tend to cry at the drop of a hat. But I also have some pretty cool powers, like my dissolving-in-water trick. And I have no trouble communicating with other Water creatures – river spirits, sprites, merpeople, and so on.

Collum was a gnome – an Earth Elemental. Earth is all about stability, steadfastness, and permanence, and I could see all that reflected in his home. Not only did it look like it was part of the landscape, it was clear that it was never going anywhere. The walls were thick and solid, the door was a generous slab of wood, and the floors were granite.

Inside, for all the heaviness in the furnishings, I noted a softer touch here and there: curtains hung over the windows and rugs covering the floors. I even spied a knitted afghan on the settee next to the fireplace. Which reminded me of Collum's knitted cap. Which made me wonder whether there was a Mrs. Barth in the picture.

I wasn't falling for him – yet. But I'd met very few other half-Elementals, and he appealed to me on the basis of being like me. Although very, very different.

So I touched the afghan and said innocently, "Who's the knitter?"

"Oh," he chuckled, "my mother made that."

"It's lovely. Very warm, I bet." I pointed at his head. "Did she make your hat, too?"

His smile grew wider. "No. I bought it at a craft fair. Please sit down. Would you like a beer?"

"Sure," I said, perching on the settee.

He disappeared into what I presumed was the kitchen and returned with two brown bottles with hand-drawn labels. "Here," he said. "I make my own."

I took a swig and smiled with pleasure. "This is really good, Collum. Why do you bother going into town for a drink when you've got your own?"

He sat in a chair across from me. "I can't make Guinness." He drank from his own bottle. "Besides, I get a little stir-crazy up here by myself. Sometimes it's good to get out and mix with people, you know?"

"Sure," I said, although I'd never really lived anywhere that I felt shut away from humanity. Mam and I had always lived near other people, and I'd always gone to public school. "Still," I said, "in some respects, I think it would be easier to live apart from other people. There's a lot smaller risk of exposure." I laughed at a memory. "Mam had a horrible time getting me exempted from gym class."

"You would have rocked swimming," he said.

"I would have, yeah. But we were required to take showers at the end of class, and she was not having it. She was sure I'd dissolve in front of the whole school."

He laughed. "That wouldn't have been a problem for me, but school would have been a challenge in other ways."

"Oh? Like what?"

"Well…I can be pretty stubborn." He glanced up at me.

"You? No way!" I laughed.

"Yes way. There was one time I didn't want to come in from recess. I was so mad at the teacher for insisting I come inside that I turned into a rock."

I laughed in disbelief. "An actual rock?"

"Yeah. It wasn't my proudest moment. It wasn't even a pretty rock — just a regular boulder like you'd see along the river."

"You could have put a bit more effort into it," I said. "You could have been marble. Or some kind of gemstone."

"I wish I'd thought of it," he said. "But I was little then. It takes practice to turn into an emerald or a ruby." He smiled shyly. "What's your favorite gemstone, Raney?"

"Aquamarine," I said.

"I should have guessed," he said. He made a fist with the hand that wasn't holding the beer bottle and shook it, his brow furrowed. Two or three seconds passed. Then he opened his hand and held it out to me. An unpolished rock of watery blue sat in the middle of his palm. "Take it," he said.

I picked it up and gazed at it. "That's amazing. Uh, you didn't give up part of you to make this, did you?"

"Nah. I pulled it to me. I have an affinity for Earth."

I smiled at his phrasing. I'd used the same words more times than I could count to explain my relationship with Water. I handed the stone back, but he said, "No, you keep it. I got it for you."

"Well, thanks," I said, and slipped it into the pocket of my slacks. "Any other talents? Besides tracking, I mean."

He ducked his head. "It's not as hard as it sounds. I just listen to the Earth. It tells me what I need to know."

"Like where Conor's body washed up, and who might be able to help you," I said – and regretted it instantly. Collum's expression had been so expansive since he'd first stepped onto the dance floor at the Private Ensign, but now his features hardened. "I'm sorry," I said. "I shouldn't have brought it up."

He waved my words away. "I miss him," he said simply. "So much." He paused, contemplating the cold hearth. "He'd been away for so long, first at college and then at graduate school. I was just a kid when he left. It felt like I grew up without him." He looked up at me. "And then he came back, and even though he didn't live here at home, we were tight. We'd text every day – goofy stuff – and we'd have supper together a couple of times a week. Sometimes he'd come here and sometimes I'd go to his place. I'd try to pet his damn cat and we'd talk about the way things ought to be." He heaved a sigh. "I've been pretty isolated out here since our parents left. It was good to have Conor back in my life. And now he's gone."

"I'm sorry," I said again.

He looked down and shook his head. "It's okay. But thanks." He looked up. "And I know you're going to find out who killed him."

"I'm going to do my best," I said. "I'm sure someone is covering up something. I'd like to know who it is, and why."

"You're a good person, Raney," he said.

"Don't get all mushy on me, Collum," I warned jokingly. "If you start crying, it'll make me puddle up. Literally."

He chuckled and swiped his wrist at his eyes. "We can't have that. If you ruin this rug, Mam will come back here and neither of us will have any peace." His smile softened. "Thanks for coming by, Raney. It's good to have someone to talk to."

"It is," I said. "Thanks for the beer."

"Any time." He walked me to the front door and paused. "Well."

"Well?" I raised my hands in a shrug.

He took it as a sign and enveloped me in a bear hug. Then he sort of sprang back. "Sorry! I didn't mean…"

I grinned. "Goodnight, Collum. I'll let you know if I find out anything else."

He opened the door and I stepped through it. Then I turned. "Uh, Collum?"

"Yeah?"

"Where am I?"

"Oh! Sorry." He walked me to the gate and held it open for me. "Head that way," he said, pointing left and uphill. "You'll find it."

"Thanks," I said, and stepped out onto the road. When I turned to wave at him, there was nothing behind me but darkness.

I wasn't all that surprised. His family had probably warded the place against prying human eyes decades – maybe even centuries – ago. Still, I had the sense that I was walking out of fairyland and into the world of men.

The moon had barely risen when I'd arrived at the bar, but now it was nearly set. It hadn't seemed like I'd been at Collum's for very long, but time moved differently across the barrier. I considered myself lucky that I hadn't lost a day or several.

I had never bothered with setting wards at my place. I'd always figured that using a stage name was misdirection enough.

Mam gave me a hard time for it, though. "When have you ever known me to neglect setting a ward at any place where we've lived?" she'd said, the first time she visited me in L.A.

"I don't feel the need to hide from my father," I'd shot back. Because that was why she'd always warded our home — so my father couldn't find us and take her back with him. She needed her independence, she always said. But I'd always suspected that she only stayed with him long enough to get pregnant and deliver a healthy baby — one, as she would always say, with a soul. "Anyway," I'd gone on, "I couldn't have set wards in college. I always had a roommate — she wouldn't have been able to lift them. And other people were in and out of our room all the time. Wards would have been impractical."

"So you let your guard down for a few years and didn't get caught," she said. "So now you think it's all right."

I had no answer for her. Or anyway, not one she would like. The truth was that I'd fallen out of the habit at college — and nothing bad *had* happened.

But here in this lovely but transient abode — a two-room suite on the first floor of a converted Victorian-era house in the Upper Town — I wondered whether I ought to get back in the habit of setting wards. I stopped for a moment at the threshold and set a minor one — just enough to make someone think twice about entering if he or she had no business being here. I didn't want to keep the owner from getting in, after all.

Collum's home was overtly Earthy, but my place in L.A. was not as Watery as it could be. I hadn't gone as far as installing a diving well in the bathroom, although I'd considered it. But I had a few touches here and there: the color scheme was sand and aqua, and I had a tabletop fountain running constantly. And a pool on the terrace that overlooked the Pacific Ocean. You might think I'd have an aquarium, but you'd be wrong. I didn't feel comfortable about confining living beings to a tiny tank. Fish belonged in nature, living free. As Mam would say, too many of our kind had been captured by humanity. We shouldn't do it to brethren.

My Airbnb didn't have a diving well, either, but it did have a soaking tub. It had been a long, difficult day, and the euphoria of the evening had begun to wear off. I shed my clothes on my way to the bathroom and eased myself blissfully into the tub as it filled.

The soak replenished me, but I was no closer to having answers about either our floater or Alex Drake. Or for that matter, about Collum Barth.

The following morning, I was nursing a second cup of coffee and reading the paper online when my cell phone rang. "Raney? It's Gail Oleander," said the voice on the other end of the line. "We met at the Private Ensign last night."

"Of course," I said, recalling the tin whistle player with the flowing top. "How are you, Gail?"

"All right," she said. "You and the leprechaun disappeared in a hurry last night. One moment you were there, and the next – poof! You'd vanished!" She laughed as she said it. "We wondered where you'd gone so fast."

I laughed in turn. "Well, he didn't show me his pot of gold, if that's what you're asking," I said. "What can I do for you?"

"Well." She hesitated. "You know how we were discussing the possible project on Virginius Island?"

I sat up straighter, remembering that she worked for the Park Service. "Yes?"

"I asked around this morning, and I learned a little bit about it."

"Where are you? I can be there in less than ten minutes."

"Oh, I don't want to meet here," she said. "I mean, not right now. How about if we have lunch in the Lower Town? In, say, an hour?"

"Sure, that would be fine."

She named a sandwich shop near the Amtrak station and I promised to be there.

Gail was waiting at an outdoor table when I got to the restaurant. I almost didn't recognize her – she'd exchanged her gauzy top of the night before for a brown Park Service shirt, and her long, graying blond hair was caught up in a no-nonsense bun at the nape of her neck. "Sorry I'm late," I said, sliding onto the bench across from her.

"No worries. I just got here myself. I hope sitting outdoors is okay with you. I like to get fresh air whenever I can."

"Sure, this is fine."

An awkward silence followed as we perused our menus and decided what to order. Once the waitress had come and gone, I looked at her and said, "So."

"So." She spread her fingers on the wooden table. "I nosed around a little bit this morning – listened here and there, you know. And it sounds like this development on Virginius Island is going to be a big deal."

"How big?"

"Bringing industry back to the island. *That* big."

I shook my head. "It sounds crazy, from what you guys were saying last night."

"I know. But apparently there's interest in redeveloping water power, since it's a renewable resource. The island would be a demonstration project. They would build the hydroelectric plant first, and then some kind of heavy industry." She leaned forward and lowered her voice. "I hope it's not weapons. I mean, it would be historically accurate. Hall's Island, which is just upriver from Virginius, was home to a rifle factory in the 1800s. But John Hall made breech-loading rifles. Technology has come a long way since then."

She sat back. "But I think this project will have something to do with agriculture." She shook her head. "I think. The plans sound kind of vague."

The waitress brought our food just then, and we dug in. "Thanks for letting me know," I said between mouthfuls of my chicken salad sandwich. "But didn't you guys say the island is prone to flooding? What are they going to do about that?"

"Something about infill."

"Raising the level of the island, you mean?" She nodded, and I pondered that for a moment. "I wonder what impact that would have here on the Lower Town. I'd think the damage from flooding would be worse if the islands were more of a barrier."

Gail shrugged. "You'd need someone who knows more about water than I do to answer that question."

As it happens, I know someone who knows a lot about water. Several someones, in fact. I made a mental note to ask Shenandoah herself what the impact of a higher barrier island would be on the Lower Town. Aloud, I said, "Well, thanks, anyway. You've given me some ideas for where to go next."

She smiled. "You're welcome. Oh, I forgot to tell you: The developer is working with the Park Service and Jefferson County. So there wouldn't be any records of it at Town Hall."

I blinked. "Thanks, Gail. So I'd have to go to the county seat? Where's that?"

"Charles Town. It's not far. Let me know if you need a ride. I could take you on my day off."

"Thanks," I said again. "I appreciate the offer."

"And please let me know if you need any other information. I'm pretty good at catching wind of things."

Another person who phrased things oddly. First Collum and his Earthy turns of phrase, and now Gail with her ability to pick up information from the wind. And there was the blowsy top she'd had on the night before. I frowned slightly. Did we have a convention of Elementals? And if Collum was Earth and Gail was Air, who was Fire? And why were we all gathered here, right now?

"Everything okay, Raney?" Gail asked.

"Yup, everything's fine." I grinned, although I felt less than merry just then.

CHAPTER 5 – WEDNESDAY AFTER LUNCH

We didn't linger long over lunch. Gail had to get back to work, and anyway, I rapidly tired of making small talk with her, skirting around all the questions I would have asked her if I'd known her better: What do you know about the Elements? Do you have any idea how Airy you seem to me?

Clouds had begun to gather while we ate. "Looks like rain," Gail observed as we gathered up our trash.

"It does, doesn't it?" I wrapped my half-eaten sandwich in a napkin and shoved it into my pack. "I thought August was pretty dry in this part of the country."

She laughed and pushed open the door. "Depends on your definition of dry. It gets quite humid, but I guess you've already figured that part out." At my nod, she went on, "Sometimes we get a thunderstorm in the afternoon. Sometimes it washes the humidity from the air. More often than not, though, it gets more humid after the storm ends." She shook her head as she went through the doorway ahead of me, then held it open so I could join her on the narrow landing.

"Sounds pleasant," I said.

"I hate summers here," she confided as we climbed the steps to the street. "The air gets so heavy. I feel like it's pinning me to the ground."

There it was again – that odd Elemental turn of phrase. I opened my mouth to remark on it, but a rumble of thunder gave me pause. It might not have been a warning, but I thought it best not to take the chance. Instead I said, "Thanks for the company at lunch. And thanks for the information."

"Any time," she said. Casting a wary eye at the sky, she went on, "I need to scoot. My umbrella's back at the office." She glanced sideways at me. "You didn't bring one, by any chance, did you?"

I shrugged. "Nope. But this jacket is pretty much waterproof. I'll be fine."

"I'm sure you will," she said. "Well. Don't float away."

"I'll do my best," I said. And then, as a breeze sprang up, I added, "Don't let the wind blow you off-course."

She gave me a grand smile and left without another word.

I watched her head downhill to the Park Service offices. Then I slowly shook my head and turned uphill, back toward my place.

The breeze chased me to the Upper Town, and the first drops of rain hit me as I neared the turn for the house. Suddenly, I had no interest in hiding away from a perfectly good thunderstorm. I raised the hood of my jacket, more for form's sake than from any desire to avoid getting wet, and kept walking.

I didn't have a particular destination in mind, and yet my feet seemed to know where they were carrying me. As the rain began coming down in earnest, I saw a sign saying, *Welcome to Bolivar*. It occurred to me that if I wanted to check out Conor's place, this might be the best time to do it – fewer people would be out in a thunderstorm, and those who were would be more interested in getting in out of the wet than in whatever some random hiker might be doing.

Conor had lived in a small, brick Cape Cod on a street full of small, brick Cape Cods. But it wasn't hard to tell which one was his – the county police had strung yellow caution tape around the arbor, overgrown with wisteria, that served as a gateway to the house. *Nothing discreet about the cops around here, is there?* I snorted to myself, ducked under the tape and into the shelter of the arbor – and pulled up short. I couldn't go any farther.

I could enter the little structure without any trouble, and it seemed to be okay for me to take shelter there. But something discouraged me from stepping through to the other side. Even the thought of pressing on gave

40

me the creeps. And at the same time, I had a strong sense that there was nothing of value inside. Better to just keep moving. In fact, it would be best if I forgot I was ever here.

What on earth…?

Oh. Earth. Duh. The place is warded. If Collum was half-gnome, his brother would have been, too. Apparently I was the only Elemental who didn't think her home turf was worth protecting.

The question now was whether I could sidestep Conor's ward in order to get in. If it was similar to the cantrip I'd put on my own front door, it was only meant to discourage entry, not to prevent it entirely. If discouragement was the goal, usually some determined probing could break it. If prevention was what he had been after…well, breaking it was going to hurt.

The rain was coming down harder, which made it more plausible to any nosy neighbors that I continued to stand in the archway while I sized up the task at hand. I stood with my back to the street and with my hands held in the traditional gesture of supplication, palms up, I felt for the ward's edges. It's hard to explain what I was looking for, but if you've ever held your hand out of the window of a moving vehicle, you'll have a sense of what I was after – a repellant force, like a cushion of air pushing me steadily away.

I found the edge on one side, and then on the other. As I'd suspected, it was meant to be discouraging. Moreover, it had been set some time ago and hadn't recently been renewed. Breaking it would be a simple matter of tugging the edge where it had begun to fray and…

There. The ward collapsed in on itself with a puff of etheric dust. It really *had* been there for a long time.

Typical guy. No sense of why housekeeping is so important. I stepped confidently through the gap where the discouraging ward had recently been, and *wham!* I hit a wall that knocked me back into the arbor, where the vines overhead dumped more water on me than I would have thought it possible for them to hold.

41

The dousing didn't bother me – water was my Element, after all, and anyway I was already soaked. I righted myself and stared intently at this second ward, as if I could tell anything about it from merely looking at it. Cautiously, with supplicating hands up, I approached it again and took its measure. It was newer by far – set within the past twenty-four hours, unless I missed my guess – and it felt different. Magical creatures have a signature feel – sort of like an etheric perfume – and I could tell this new ward hadn't been set by Conor because the signature was different from the ward that had frayed away. Besides, it was too new for him to have set it – he'd been dead for longer than a day. But it didn't have the feel of the ward around Collum's home, either. This felt alien. Maybe not even human.

I cocked my head and approached it again, feeling for that alien perfume. Then I stepped back and scratched my head with a damp forefinger.

The cat?

I mean, if it wasn't Conor's and it wasn't Collum's, there weren't many other candidates. And then there was the shower the wisteria had given me. That was a total cat move.

But Collum should have picked it up by now. Why hadn't he?

And why would the cat feel the need to fortify the ward? Unless the police had done a number on the interior of the house…

"Here, kitty, kitty, kitty," I called, clicking my tongue against my teeth. "Nice kitty. I'm a good person. A helper. I won't mess anything up, I promise." When the cat didn't appear, I added, "I'm a friend of Collum's."

And why would that make me feel any more charitable toward you? The voice was bored, with an undercurrent of hostility. I had a mental picture of an orange tabby regarding me with feigned disinterest, wielding an emery board to file a claw to razor sharpness.

"He asked me to stop by," I said.

Pfft. The sound of filing grew louder.

"I can feed you. I have opposable thumbs."

The filing stopped. *Tuna?* the cat asked hopefully.

42

I shrugged off my pack and pulled out my half-eaten sandwich, shielding it from the weather as best I could. "Would chicken do?"

There's stuff on it.

"It's mayonnaise," I said. "Look, how about I give you this for now, you let me in, and I'll bring you a whole can of tuna?"

No deal. You might not come back.

A fair point from the cat's perspective. "All right. How about this: I give you this, you let me in, and I find the guy who killed Conor?"

Is that *why you're here? Why didn't you say so in the first place?* The ward dropped abruptly. I took advantage of it and dashed to the house, in case the cat changed its mind.

The front door opened as I reached the porch. I stepped inside and closed the door, then shed my pack and jacket. Immediately, I was beset by piteous meowing, as an orange tabby queen, shaped like a beach ball, rubbed herself against my legs. *Where's that chicken, sister?*

I dropped to the floor and sat cross-legged while I unwrapped the sandwich. "My name's Raney," I said as the cat chowed down. "What's yours?"

Tiger.

I chuckled. "Needless to say."

She paused and regarded me. *It's not my real name. But it's what Conor called me. And you're not using your real name, either. Are you?*

Our gazes locked for a moment. Then she went back to eating my sandwich.

"Okay," I said. "Let's put all the cards on the table. Why are there so many Elementals gathered here right now? And what do you know about this ancient evil that Shenandoah mentioned?"

She nibbled daintily at the last few morsels of meat, then sat back and began to groom her whiskers. *I don't speak with river gods,* she said irritably, as if I should have known better.

"Oh, right. You're a cat." I grinned wickedly. "Which is why you thought that bucket of water over the arbor was a stroke of genius."

She paused, her eyes round. *Oh.* She went back to washing herself. *It was mostly there for Collum, anyway.*

"What do you have against him? He seems like a nice guy."

He's a gnome.

"So was Conor, wasn't he? They were brothers, right?"

Conor was different. She stopped washing herself and stalked away.

I realized I was being an insensitive ass. "Hey, Tiger, I'm sorry. I know you miss him."

He never said goodbye. Just left me with a bowlful of kibble and a promise to clean my litter box when he got back. She turned her back on me.

"It's not like he meant to disappear," I said. "Somebody killed him."

I figured that out when those men came in.

I frowned. "The cops?"

No, they came later. This was before.

"Okay," I said. I realized I was going to have to reconstruct a timeline with a cat who basically never knew what time of day it was unless somebody pulled out a can opener. "So one day, Conor left. Was it morning? Was it his usual time to leave?"

Yes, it was morning. And he was in a hurry. That's why he didn't scoop my box.

"Okay. Leaving aside the litter box…"

He always *scoops my box every morning.*

"Ah, okay. So he was in a *big* hurry."

She turned around and blinked at me. I guessed that qualified as a kitty head nod.

"So how long after he left did these other men come in? The ones who weren't cops, I mean."

I knew who you meant. She turned away again. *I didn't like them. They were loud. And they overturned things in Conor's office.*

I started. What a lousy investigator I was – I should be looking for damage or for something the intruders missed, and instead I was having a conversation with a cat. Then again, the cat was a witness. "I'll go look in a minute. Right now, I'm trying to figure out when the men arrived. Was it dark when they came? Or maybe it got dark and then light again?"

Again came the kitty snort. *I understand the concept of day and night. It was the same day, but it was after suppertime. When I heard the key turn in the lock, I thought it was Conor, and I went to the door to give him a piece of my mind for being late. But it wasn't him.* She fell silent and turned away again.

"I'm sorry," I said again. "That must have been very hard for you. Did they take anything away with them?"

I don't know! I didn't see them leave. I was hiding behind the... She eyed me over one shoulder. *In my safe space. I stayed in my safe space until they were gone.*

"Don't worry," I said. "I won't tell anyone where your safe space is." I held my hand out tentatively. "Pets?"

She practically rushed me. I gave her a good scratching around her neck and between her ears, and she began purring madly. "So," I went on quietly, "Collum said he and Conor had dinner on Wednesday night. Was it Thursday morning that Conor left in a rush?"

Yes, she purred.

"And the intruders let themselves in Thursday night. With Conor's key." I kept scratching and she kept purring. I took that as a yes. "So the police must have come by on Sunday."

Two days.

My hand stilled. "Two days would be Saturday. The police came Saturday?"

Yes. But they didn't wrap the arbor until the next day.

"But that doesn't make any sense. What reason would the cops have to come by the day before I found Conor's body?"

Tiger pulled away. *You found him?*

"He was already dead," I said gently. "I was hiking through. Shenandoah left his body along the bank for me to find."

Why you?

"That's what I'd like to know." I sighed. "She said it has something to do with this ancient evil I asked you about before. I'm supposed to stop it somehow." I sighed again and unfolded my legs. "Come on. I'll take a look at the office, and then I'll scoop your box. Deal?"

In response, she paced off down the hall. *This way.*

Collum's office was off the kitchen. It must have originally been the garage; I stepped through an archway and down to a floor covered in indoor-outdoor carpet with not much cushioning underneath. Conor, or whoever put down the carpet for him, must have laid it right over the original concrete floor.

IKEA bookcases lined the long wall opposite the entrance, and a large table took up the middle of the room. I assumed the shelves usually held books and the table typically held blueprints and things, but nearly all of it was jumbled together on the floor. To my right was a wall of windows that gave an expansive view of Conor's backyard, the back of a neighbor's house, and the tree-covered hillside beyond. A white countertop ran the length of that wall and must have served as Conor's desk, but that, too, had been searched – office supplies were scattered across the counter, their containers overturned. An old-fashioned slanted architect's desk stood to the right – or would have, if it hadn't had a leg broken off in the ruckus. His upholstered desk chair, too, had been ruined, the leather slashed and pulled back to reveal the guts underneath.

I let out an explosive sigh. "I don't even know where to begin to look," I said.

Tiger crossed the room and went under the counter to the farthest corner. There she sat and looked at me with glowing eyes.

"Hiding won't help," I told her.

Humans are so dumb, she said, and pointedly looked up.

"Oh! Sorry." I approached her hidey-hole and got down on all fours. She got out of my way so I could crawl all the way back into the corner and look up.

Sure enough, something was stuck to the underside of the counter with duct tape. I had just peeled the tape off the counter when a voice bellowed, "What the hell are you doing in here?"

Startled, I scooted out and sat up at the same time, banging my head on the edge of the counter. "Ow."

"Raney?"

I rubbed my head and blinked. "Collum?"

He stood under the arch, the shoulders of his jacket dotted with raindrops. Beads of water glistened in his beard. He scowled at Tiger, who growled low in her throat. "You let her in but you blocked me?"

She brought me chicken, she responded, still growling.

"Is it still raining?" I asked him.

"It's letting up. I decided I'd better come over and try again to pick up this ungrateful creature," he said, which earned him a hiss.

"Um," I said. "I'm going to get some ice for my head." I got up, wincing, and passed between the two of them, heading for the refrigerator. I put down the duct-taped thing on the tiny island and pulled a paper towel from the roll on the counter, then turned toward the fridge – but Collum beat me. He had pulled a ziplock bag from a drawer and deposited a couple of ice cubes into it.

"So it doesn't drip all over," he said, holding the bag out to me.

"Thanks." I wrapped the makeshift cold pack in the paper towel and applied it to my head.

"Sorry I startled you."

"It's fine."

He picked up the tape. "What's this?"

"No idea. I'd just found it when you came in."

He pulled off the tape. "It's a thumb drive." We traded a look, and then Collum went back to the threshold of his brother's office. "His laptop is gone."

He took it when he left.

"Conor took it?" I asked. She blinked slowly. I turned to Collum. "So whoever killed him must have it. But they didn't find what they needed on it, so they came here to look for it. Scared the heck out of poor Tiger, too."

"Oh, sure. You let *them* in," he said to the cat in a wounded tone.

I didn't know! I thought it was Conor coming home!

"They used his key to get in," I said. "Seriously, what is the deal between you two?"

"We have a history," he said. "But she needs to come home with me."

Not a chance. I'm staying put.

"You can't," Collum said. "Conor's not coming back. We're going to have to put the house on the market." He looked toward the ceiling. "Look at me, arguing with a cat."

"How about we have this discussion later?" I said. "I came here to figure out who killed Conor. That's what you asked me to do, right? And you're literally holding a clue I just found." I leaned back against the counter, still holding the ice pack against my head. "Now if we were on a TV show, the next thing we'd do is find a computer to plug it into, so we could find out what's on it. Right?"

"Right," said Collum.

"Have you got one?"

"With me? No. But we could *all* go to my place…"

Nuh-uh. Nice try, forest boy. Tiger gave several emphatic tail swishes.

"Or my place," I said.

Collum looked at me in surprise. "You brought a laptop with you to hike the A.T.?"

"Of course not," I said. "The place I'm staying has a desktop for guests to use."

"Let's go, then," he said.

"Hang on a minute," I said. "I promised Tiger I'd scoop her box before I left."

CHAPTER 6 – STILL WEDNESDAY

Tiger opted to stay home. I prevailed upon Collum to let her win, for now. He grumbled, but acquiesced.

The rain had stopped by the time we left. As soon as we stepped through the arbor, I felt the ward slam up behind us. We traded a look of surprise. "That was emphatic," Collum said.

"It's probably not a bad idea," I said. "We don't have any other way to keep an eye on the place for now."

"As long as she lets us back in."

Bring tuna.

I laughed out loud. Collum shot a scowl toward the house.

A few minutes later, I was lowering my own ward to let him in my place. He glanced at me. "General all-purpose stuff, huh? I could help you with setting a stronger one."

"Thanks, but I know how," I said, rather frostily. "I didn't see the point." I unlocked the mundane lock and turned the knob. "Of course, that was before I found that thing you're holding. Come on in."

He preceded me into the apartment. "Nice," he said appreciatively, looking around.

"It's fine," I said, holding out my hand for his jacket. He shrugged out of it, and I hung both his and mine, side by side, in the coat closet. "My house in L.A. is bigger, but this beats a hut on the A.T."

"I suppose your place in L.A. is on the water," he said.

"Beach house, yeah. In Malibu."

"Of course. You and the rest of the movie stars."

I frowned. "What's that supposed to mean?"

He sighed and perched on the edge of an easy chair. "I don't know. This is all kind of weird for me. I don't mix much with people." He placed a tentative hand on an armrest. "I come into town for session night to have a beer. Sometimes I have dinner with my brother. And now…" He shrugged. "Now Conor's gone and everywhere I go, I'm running into a movie star."

"TV," I said.

"Close enough. It's just weird, that's all." He watched his hand on the armrest. "You probably have a posse back home."

I shouted a laugh. "Not exactly. I dissolve in water, remember?"

He looked up at me archly. "I do."

My face suddenly felt aflame. "Okay! Well, let's see what's on that thumb drive." I turned and led him to the counter space off the kitchen where the owner had installed the "business center" – a desktop computer of fairly recent vintage, an inkjet printer, and the wi-fi router.

I fired up the computer and held out my hand for the drive. He pulled me into his arms and planted his mouth on mine.

I should maybe have been shocked or angry that he'd come on so strong, so soon. But undine emotions are triggered by all sorts of things – including sex. We're always raring to go. And magical genetics give Elementals the sort of protection against disease that mortals would love to have. So when Collum made his move, I was ready to meet it.

It had been some time since I'd kissed a man with a beard. The ex had preferred the clean-shaven look, although he'd cycled through all sorts of facial hairstyles for his various roles. He'd never had a full beard, though. Collum's was nice. Cushy. Not as scratchy as I'd expected it to be.

I'd also never kissed another Elemental before. Mam had kept me away from even our own kind. Better to blend in as human, she would say to me. It will make you harder to spot.

But intimacy with a full human had always felt off to me – like I was playing a role. Like my partner was expecting something from me that I couldn't fully give. It made me wary of relationships in general. I felt like I would always disappoint the other person involved.

I had certainly disappointed the ex. He got mad at me after I refused to make money off of the fact that I was an undine. At least, that's what his problem seemed to be. You never know, though. People make excuses sometimes. They say one thing to avoid saying the thing they really ought to say.

What I ought to be saying right now, I guess, is that in Collum's arms, I didn't feel that lack. His human half and my human half were the same. His Elemental half complemented mine: Water and Earth, while fundamentally different, blend pretty well. Not like Water and Fire, say — Water quenches Fire. And Air carries Water. But Earth and Water…

Well, okay, Earth and Water make mud. But there's strength in mud. Just ask the people around the world who build their homes out of it.

He was substantial, strong. I flowed around him. And it was much, much later when we finally got around to looking at the contents of that thumb drive.

"He never told me about this," Collum said quietly.

We'd been staring at the computer screen for several minutes, taking it all in. The information Conor had hidden away — that he'd given his life for — was only tangentially related to the construction planned for Virginius Island.

"This is bad," Collum said. "This is really bad." He sat heavily on the dinette chair nearest the computer.

"Where is this?" I asked. "The area doesn't look anything like any of the maps I studied while I was planning my hike."

"I'm not surprised," he said. "This region isn't on typical topo maps."

I frowned. "Is it in West Virginia?"

"Yes and no. Here, let me drive for a minute." I scooted the rolling desk chair over so he could type standing up. He brought up a satellite map of the area near Harpers Ferry and zoomed in to a part that looked uninhabited. "A lot of West Virginia's traditional industry centers around the mining of coal and other minerals. You've heard about that, I'm sure."

51

I nodded. "I've also heard that coal's heyday is pretty much over."

"That's true. The seams that were easy to get to are mostly played out, and anyway the fashion now is for cleaner energy sources. We're getting there. West Virginia has three wind farms already."

"That's good news."

"It's huge for a state where coal has been king for so long. But not everybody is ready to let go of the old ways." He pulled his chair over and sat down again. "And there's still coal in these hills. It's just harder to get to." He glanced at the screen. "Some of it should never be dug out. But whoever's behind this project is determined to do it."

"I'm not sure what you're saying. Is this coal inaccessible? Too expensive to mine? What?"

He looked at me speculatively for a moment. "Do you know what a wight is?"

I knew. My eyes widened. "There's a *wight* trapped in these hills?"

"Well," Collum said, leaning back and interlacing his fingers across his belly, "I wouldn't say it's *trapped*, exactly. But its area of influence, you could say, has been restricted." He stood up again and expanded the area the map covered, so that Harpers Ferry was visible again. "This area is special. It's a liminal place. It spans two realities."

"I thought so," I said. "The confluence of the two rivers makes it so."

He grinned at me. "I suppose it *would* look that way from an undine's perspective. But there's more to it than that." He took a breath and intoned, "The mountains reach deep into the earth. Their roots touch the fire at the earth's core. Water, too, springs from deep in the earth. And the trees nurtured by the mountains create the air we breathe."

It sounded like a catechism. "I suppose it would look that way from a gnome's perspective," I said, arching my eyebrows.

His mouth quirked up at one corner. Then he kissed me. "Anyway," he resumed, "you get the idea. All the Elements are here, in such abundance that they reach across dimensions."

My brain caught the undercurrent of what he was saying. "So the wight's not in this dimension," I said.

"Right. It was here long before man came to this land. It may have been created when the earth was created. Anyway, it found a way to coexist with the Native Americans who lived here – or maybe it would be more accurate to say *they* found a way to coexist with *it*. They set an informal boundary out of respect for the wight's power, and in exchange the wight made sure they had everything they needed to survive."

"And then the white man came," I said.

He nodded. "And they were a whole lot less respectful of the wight's personal space. They wanted more and more land. More and more natural resources. Just…more."

"So the wight fought back?"

"Landslides. Earthquakes. Disasters of all types." He re-centered the map on Harpers Ferry. "My father used to talk about the floods that destroyed the rifle factory on Hall's Island. This town was poised to take off back then. We had the industry and the river access, and our population was growing. But then floodwaters washed it all away. Da blamed the wight for it." He glanced at me. "He was joking, of course. It couldn't have been – the wight had been sequestered long before."

"How?" I asked. "How did you guys get the wight to this other dimension? I mean, I presume it was the gnomes who trapped it."

"We had help," he said, "but it was our idea. That's what the legend says, anyway. But I know one part of it is true for sure: there's a gateway up in those hills."

"A gateway to the wight's dimension."

"Uh-huh." He flipped the screen back to Conor's diagram and pointed. "Right about there. A waterfall marks the spot. I've been up there. It's pretty. I went one time with…" He flushed and broke off his reminiscing.

"Someone special?" I asked.

"She was something," he admitted. "But she wasn't as special as you."

"Uh-huh," I said with a smile. "Hold that thought. What about this waterfall?"

He cleared his throat. "Well. The wight is guarding the last truly workable seam of coal in the state. It's a big one, and it's mostly in this other dimension that the wight has been restricted to. The waterfall is the gateway to this other dimension, like I said, and it's heavily warded." He tapped the computer screen. "And it's right there where these idiots are planning to dig."

"I imagine that would let the wight out," I said.

"I imagine you're right."

"I imagine that would be bad for humanity."

"It wouldn't be so great for Elementals, either," he said. "We're the ones who trapped it."

I blew out a breath. "So the ideal would be to stop the project. But I guess that's what Conor tried to do."

Collum looked at his feet. "Yeah."

"And Plan B would be – what? Gather a team of Elementals to coop up the wight somewhere else?

"Where, though?" he asked. "And where are we gonna find a team?"

"I'm pretty sure I know where we can find a sylph." I told him about my lunch with Gail Oleander.

He nodded thoughtfully. "I thought there was something Airy about her when we met her the other night. So assuming you're right about her..."

"We'd need to find a salamander. Do you know any?"

He shrugged. "Nope. But I didn't know you until a couple of days ago. Maybe the Universe will provide us with one."

I eyed him skeptically. "You think so?"

He came over to me and pulled me up out of the chair and into his arms. "It brought you here to me, didn't it?"

"Mmm," I said. "And I've been thinking it brought *you* to *me*."

I would have been okay with Collum staying the night, but he declined. "There's stuff I have to do in the morning," he said.

"What stuff?"

"Chores."

"What chores?"

"Just, you know. Chores." He rolled out of bed and started to get dressed. "What are your plans for tomorrow?"

"Chores," I said shortly.

He looked back at me. Then he dropped the jeans he had been about to put on and sat back down on the bed near me. "I'm sorry. There's just stuff I have to do around the house, that's all. Part of my routine."

"And it can't be done later in the day."

"I don't..." He raised one shoulder in a shrug and looked away. Then he focused on me again. "I don't know what would happen if I let it go."

"So you're OCD?"

"Come on, Raney." He got up and picked up his jeans again.

"No, I'm serious." I threw back the covers and stood next to him. "I've never really known a gnome before. What do you do all day? Do you work? Are you a miner or something?"

He shook his head and laughed. "No, I'm not a miner."

"Well, Conor was a geologist. I thought it was a fair guess."

"It was. But I'm not." He pulled his shirt over his head.

"It has to be something Earthy..." I crossed my arms under my breasts and placed a forefinger on my chin. "I know! You're a farmer!"

"No," he said. "And if you stand there like that..."

"Like what?" I said, arching an eyebrow.

"Don't you have a robe or something?" He sat on the edge of the bed and picked up a sock. "You're very distracting."

I sat next to him and draped an arm over his shoulder, pressing close. "That's the idea."

He sighed loudly. Then he rolled his arm up over my head and kissed me, pushing me back onto the bed.

Things were looking up, you might say. Except he contrived somehow to get the sheet in between us. Then he rolled. Then he got up and left me there, swaddled in bedclothes, and resumed dressing.

"Collum! That's not fair!" I spluttered.

He laughed at me. "Oh, like what you were doing to me was fair!" He leaned over and kissed me again. "Set a ward after I'm gone. A real one this time."

I scowled at him as he left the bedroom. Then I untangled myself and followed after him. "Hey, do you want to take the thumb drive?"

He paused, one arm in his hoodie. "No," he said. "You keep it. They'll come to my place first. We'll all be better off it's not there."

"Who's they?" I said. "Conor's employer or the cops?"

"Either one," he said. "Set a ward, Raney. I'm serious." And he let himself out.

"Yeah, I got that part," I muttered, and slammed up a wall. I was beginning to understand why Tiger felt the way she did about him.

As I turned around, I realized I'd never told Collum that the cops had visited his brother's place the day before I'd found his body. And then I remembered that nice Officer Hartley had found me this lovely place with the lovely soaking tub. So if the cops thought I knew anything – anything at all – about why Conor had disappeared, they would have zero trouble tracking me down.

I turned back to the door and doubled the strength of the ward. Then I went around the house and warded all the windows, all the pipes where they came through the walls – every place, basically, where something or someone could get in or out. I also warded the wi-fi router and the TV, just in case.

Then, shaking, I ran a bath and climbed in, and lost myself in the water.

CHAPTER 7 – THURSDAY

I came awake slowly, still half-dreaming at first. I'd been walking all around a big, busy hotel, looking for Tiger. When I finally found her, she jumped into my arms and said, "Have you found the gate yet?" Her little kitty lips moved and everything.

"We should find Collum," I said. "He knows where it is."

"Of course he does. Collum *is* the gate," said Tiger.

I came awake plotting ways to get Collum to admit he was the way in. I realized I was completely awake when it occurred to me to ask myself, *the way into what?* By then, of course, dream Tiger was long gone.

I should have twigged to the dream state I was in when I didn't think it was weird that the cat was talking out loud.

I cobbled together breakfast from my rapidly-depleting supplies. I'd planned for a week's delay at the outside. Here it was, Thursday, and I'd had no calls from anyone official. I'd paid for the rental unit through Sunday morning, but if nobody needed me, I had no problem with checking out early. I'd even let the owner keep my money.

There was my extra-friendly neighborhood gnome, though, as mysterious as he'd been the night before. And Conor's cat. And I still hadn't figured out who had killed Conor himself – not really. I had a name – Alex Drake – but no proof, and only sketchy evidence that the whole thing was bigger than a dead not-kayaker.

I sighed and stirred my instant oatmeal. I supposed I should do some more investigating. I pulled up the notes app on my phone and started tapping in a list of things that needed looking into:

1. The plans for the Virginius Island project, which would require a trip to Charles Town with Gail. I wondered whether

her next day off would be before I needed to extend my reservation here.

2. The police investigation into Conor's death. Why had they visited his place on Saturday? I was worried about stirring up their interest in me while snooping around, and if the developers had bought them off, that wouldn't be healthy. Maybe I could just make a call to Officer Hartley to see whether I could be on my way. She might let drop some information that would point me in a fruitful direction.

3. Groceries, if I needed to stay longer. And I needed to get some tuna for Tiger, anyway. I'd promised.

I compared my list with my interest in intrigue so early in the morning, and opted for the grocery store. I opened another blank note to make a provisions list, and remembered I'd gotten some kind of coupon that looked slightly useful when I was there before. So I rifled through my wallet to find it.

The coupon had apparently evaporated. Maybe I'd thrown it away with the receipt. But I did find Rufus MacKay's business card.

I switched back to my to-do list and added contacting him. As a union organizer, I thought, he would have a better idea of the business structure of the Virginius Island project than most. I might even get better info by talking to him, plus it would be quicker than blowing a day on looking through the county's building permits and stuff.

Call Rufus MacKay got moved toward the top of the list. If I got nothing from him, I could still round up Gail and set up a road trip with her.

But the grocery store was still at the very top of the list. And then I'd call the cops and see what I could find out from them without giving anything away.

I'd thought I was getting a jump on the heat of the day by going early, but it was already in the mid-80s by the time I left the grocery store. I'd brought my ginormous backpack so I could pack the groceries in it for the walk back to the Airbnb. I'd learned while training for the A.T. hike that it's way easier to carry a heavy load on your back than dangling from your hands on either side.

Laden with my booty, I stepped out of the air-conditioned grocery store into what felt like a furnace. My back, under the pack, was instantly soaked with sweat. I could see heat rising from the expanse of parking lot asphalt that I needed to cross to get to the street.

"It's not going to get any cooler while you stand here waiting," I muttered, and stepped out from under the store's entrance awning into the full force of the sun.

A horn blared next to me, and I jumped. The car attached to the horn cruised past, so close that it nearly brushed me. The driver rolled down his window and yelled, "Leaving our fair city so soon, Regina?"

"Oh, hi, Allen." For behind the wheel was Allen Owings, the reporter and photographer for the local newspaper. I hooked a thumb behind my back. "I guess it does look like I'm hitting the trail, doesn't it?"

"Yeah, it does. Are you?"

"Not quite yet. The police haven't told me it's okay to leave."

"Huh." He gazed out his windshield. "I guess I'm not surprised." He turned back to me. "Hey, that pack looks heavy. You're not going to try to walk somewhere in this heat, are you?"

"It's not that bad," I tried.

It didn't work. "Hop in. I'll give you a lift."

"Oh, no, I couldn't impose…"

He was already out of the car. "It's no trouble," he said, helping me out of the pack and stowing it in the back seat. Then he held open the passenger side door for me. As I got in, he said, "Besides, I have a few questions I'd like to ask you." He grinned at my hesitation. "Just kidding. Mostly."

Rapidly, I clicked through my options. I could bolt, but the pack was already in the car – and I'd put Conor's thumb drive in the bottom of it, thinking it would be safer there than in the apartment while I was out.

I offered him a weak smile and buckled myself in.

As it turned out, I got more out of him than he got out of me. "The cops probably haven't released you because the case is still open," he said. "I checked with all of our local outfitters on Monday. Nobody had an overdue kayaker and nobody was missing a boat."

I frowned at him. "So you don't think the guy was a kayaker? Or what?"

"No idea. He could have had his own boat."

"Turn here," I said, pointing to the left.

As he executed the turn, he said, "You know what I think is really weird, though?"

"No. What?"

"There's been no report of a missing person. We have a kayak with no owner and a body that nobody can match up with a missing-person report." He glanced at me. "It's like the guy came out of nowhere. Like he was an alien or something."

"Weird," I managed.

"You can say that again. Is this the place?"

"Yep. Thanks," I said as he slowed to a stop at the curb.

"Need any help with that pack?" he asked, as I jumped from the car and wrestled the beast onto my shoulders.

"Nope, I've got it." I clicked the waist belt shut and closed the back door. "Thanks for the ride."

"Hey, no problem. Of course, now I know where you live. Maybe I'll come by later." He grinned again.

"I'm sure you're trustworthy." *Good luck getting in, mortal.* "Hey, Allen? Do you think I should call the police and see if they still need me? I'd really like to get back on the trail."

He shrugged. "I guess it couldn't hurt. Oh, by the way, here." He held out his business card.

I pocketed it. Suddenly, I was done talking to him. "Thanks again for the ride," I said, and shut the front door of his car before he could say another word.

He waved and drove off. As I waited for him to round the corner and disappear, I pulled out his card and glanced over it. Then I flipped it over. "Call me," it said in thick, black Sharpie. The phone number below that was different from the office and cell phone numbers on the front of the card. Maybe it was his home number.

"Who has a landline anymore? What a dweeb," I said, releasing my wards and letting myself into the apartment.

After I'd put everything away, I decided I didn't want to stay home to find out whether Allen Owings would make good on his suggestion – or threat – to stop by. Instead, I copied the contents of the thumb drive onto a new drive I'd just bought. Then I wiped the original drive, downloaded a bunch of Barney songs onto it, and dropped it back into the bottom of my ginormous pack. The new drive I attached to my key ring, which I shoved into the front pocket of my jeans.

Hide your valuables in plain sight, Mam always said. Her advice hadn't steered me wrong yet.

Then I went out to play tourist for the rest of the day.

My first stop, though, was the police station. I stopped at the front desk and asked for Officer Hartley.

"She's out on patrol," the woman at the desk said. "Can I help you with something?"

"Oh, well, I'm Regina Heath. The one who found the kayaker on Sunday? I've kind of been waiting to hear whether the police need anything else from me," I said. "I'm through-hiking the A.T. and I'd really like to get back on the trail."

"That would be the chief's call," she said, and picked up her phone. "Chief, Regina Heath is here. You want to talk to her?... Okay. I'll tell her." She hung up and looked at me. "He said thanks for stopping by. He'll be right out. You can have a seat."

"Thanks," I said with a smile, while mentally kicking myself. *Just couldn't let sleeping dogs lie, could you?*

"Has anyone ever told you how much you look like Raney Meadows?" the woman asked.

I grinned at her. "I get that all the time, yeah."

"Oh, here he is," she said as Chief Coburn emerged from his office.

"Ms. Heath, is it?" he asked, offering me his hand to shake. "Craig Coburn."

"I know," I said. "We met at the river on Sunday."

"Of course. Won't you come in?"

I smiled faintly and followed him into his office. My trailer on the set was bigger, but he swaggered more.

"I'm glad you stopped by, Ms. Heath," he said as we got situated. "You're a hard woman to track down."

"Oh? I'm surprised. Officer Hartley knew where I was."

"Did she?"

"Yes, she did," I said evenly. "She recommended the Airbnb to me. She said her friend owns it. She even called to set up the reservation for me."

"I see," he said. He had picked up a pen from his desk and began waving it rapidly back and forth between finger and thumb, so that it looked like the pen was bending. I pulled my eyes away from the optical illusion and my gaze met his. He smiled. "What I meant was we ran a check on the I.D. you gave us and it didn't turn up anything."

"That's odd," I said faintly. The guy I'd bought it from in L.A. had told me it was as fine a false I.D. as he could manufacture.

"You think so?" he said. "I think it's fake." He put the pen down and leaned forward. "So I asked myself, 'Why would a pretty lady like Ms. Heath be using a fake I.D. to hike the Appalachian Trail?'"

"Did you answer yourself?" I asked. Nerves have always made me snarky.

"I did," he said. "I figured you were likely a criminal. But your stats didn't match anybody in the FBI's database. And then while I was watching TV the other night, it hit me." He pointed at me with delight. "You're Raney Meadows, aren't you?"

I ducked my head and smiled modestly. "You've caught me out, sir."

"I knew it!" he crowed. "Can I get an autograph? And maybe a picture?"

"Sure," I said. "Might as well get the whole department in on it."

"That would be great. I know Eunice is a big fan." He nearly ran to the door. "Hey, Eunice! You know who this is?"

"For real?" the woman at the front desk squealed. "I *thought* it looked like her!"

The next half-hour went by in a blur of autograph signings and selfies, as well as "talking shop" with actual cops about the fake investigations our writers made up for us every week. "You know that toxicology takes much longer to come back for real than it does on TV, don't you?" Officer Stannis said. He shared a grin with Eunice and the chief. "We always laugh about that. No offense, ma'am."

"None taken," I said lightly. "We have to compress the timeline a lot to get it all into an hour. Sometimes reality gets the boot."

They laughed at that, and I laughed with them. What else could I do?

Soon I was on my way, having made a bunch of friends on the Harpers Ferry police force but having learned no more about Conor's murder than I knew when I walked in the door. Moreover, it was going to be exponentially harder for me to do any checking into his death, because now the cops knew who I was.

I did, however, get the all-clear. I could leave town any time, Chief Coburn said – now that he knew my real identity. "Should be easy enough to track you down," he said. "Just call Hollywood, right?"

I smiled weakly. "Sure."

"And I'll send Cindy by to see you when she gets back from patrol," he said. "She'll bust a gut when she finds out that she had a real movie star in her cruiser."

"TV," I muttered, but I kept smiling as I thanked them all for the warm welcome. And as I walked out of the building, I realized I was going to have to tell Collum I was quitting his investigation. Too many people here knew who I was now.

My heart sank. I couldn't do it. I cared about him too much to disappoint him.

My emotions whirling, I walked through the Lower Town to the city park that overlooks the confluence of the Potomac and Shenandoah rivers. It was still hot as blazes, but the breeze off the water cooled my skin and raised my spirits a little.

And then they sank right back down. For in the river to my right, I saw a green, long-haired face, bobbing in and out of view. Soon she was joined by a similar face on the left. Even though hundreds of feet of air and mist separated us, I could hear their pleas.

I realized that I couldn't quit. It wasn't just to Collum that I'd promised to find Conor's murderer; I'd given my word to the river goddesses, too. And it would be a bad idea for an undine to go back on her word to a Water deity.

CHAPTER 8 – THE REST OF THURSDAY, AND FRIDAY

I figured I had, at most, twenty-four hours before everybody in town knew who I was. If I were going to find Conor's killer and avenge the violation of Shenandoah's waters, I was going to have to work fast.

So naturally, I went back to the apartment to take a bath. After all, I do my best thinking when I'm one with Water.

When I got there, I was dismayed – but not surprised – to find someone had tried to break in. My wards had held fine. But my would-be intruder had a human scent – and he appeared to be a fan of brute force, to boot. When he couldn't jimmy the lock on the front door, he used a crowbar on the kitchen window. I noted scuff marks on the wooden frame. I also noticed the brick laying in the grass where it had landed after he threw it at the window and it bounced off.

I picked up the brick and placed it neatly back in place in the flower bed edging where it belonged. Then I went inside, locked the door, and double-checked all the windows. Everything was still intact. I was as safe as I could be. But I was shaking as I lowered myself into the tub. As I dissolved, my trembling made the water look like it was boiling.

I mean, I kind of felt sorry for the guy. He couldn't even complete a simple breaking-and-entering job because some girl with magical powers had put an impermeable barrier around her house.

On the other hand, I felt like I'd been violated. It was a familiar sensation – one honed through years of the experience of coming home to discover Mam packing because my father had tracked us down once again. My gut reaction was to flee – but this time I couldn't run. I had made promises, and I intended to keep them.

Anyway, this wasn't like my father. He preferred mind games over physical attacks. His usual trick was to leave his business card stuck in the door frame. Crowbars weren't his style at all.

But if it wasn't dear old Dad, then who? My ex-boyfriend?

Or maybe Callum's dead brother's employer had followed me home.

Or maybe it wasn't any of them. Maybe word had gotten around about my identity quicker than I'd expected, and some idiotic paparazzo had thought he could get a perfect shot of me from inside the house.

I dismissed that right away. I also dismissed the idea that it was the ex – he would be more likely to plant a rumor than heave a brick through a window. It would mess up his manicure.

That left Conor's employer. Or the Harpers Ferry cops, I supposed, although I could account for the whereabouts of nearly everyone in the department during the time period in question. Everybody but Cindy Hartley, and she hadn't struck me as a gumshoe – she was more the traffic cop type.

Whoever it had been, though, they hadn't succeeded – nor were they likely to in the future, as long as I kept protecting myself.

Calmed by that thought, I pulled myself together, got out of the tub, and went into the bedroom to get dressed. I grabbed up the jeans I'd worn earlier – and when I did, something fell out of one of the pockets. It was about the size of a business card, and I shivered in panic, thinking maybe my father had figured out a way in, after all.

But it wasn't Dad's card. It belonged to Rufus MacKay, the red-haired fiddler. Since Rufus was organizing Alex Drake's employees – or trying to, anyway – he might have inside info on whether Drake had sent a goon or two after me. And if he didn't know for sure, he might be able to point me in the direction of someone who did.

Rufus had invited me to call him if I wanted a tour of Drake's operation. That still sounded like way more fun than poring over dusty tomes in some obscure county office in Charles Town. So first thing Friday morning, I gave him a call.

"Who is this?" he barked into the phone. I could hear shouting behind him.

"Hi, Rufus, it's Regina Heath," I said, pausing for a split second before giving him my name. "We met at the Private Ensign on Tuesday."

"Oh, right," he said, more subdued. "You were with the leprechaun."

"He's a gnome, actually," I said. I don't know what prompted me to tell the truth, but I did.

I'd expected either surprise or laughter, but Rufus shrugged it off. "Same difference," he said. "What can I do for you?"

"I mentioned Tuesday night that I'm looking for information on Alex Drake. You said you'd be willing to show me around his operation. So I was calling to see when might be a good time."

The shouting increased. "Today's not good," he said, raising his voice above the ambient noise. "We're having a bit of an argument with some of his goons."

I shuddered involuntarily. "I may have some history with them myself."

In the background, I heard what sounded like a scuffle, then a bang, and then all went ominously quiet. "Rufus?" I asked.

"Yeah, I'm here. I had to shut the door." He paused again. "Let's do it tomorrow. Do you know the diner off Wilson Freeway?"

"I can find it."

"Let's meet there around seven. We can get breakfast and head out here afterward."

"Sounds good. See you then."

He ended the call before I was able to get the phone away from my ear. I blinked in surprise. But then I decided to give him the benefit of the doubt. *Must be the situation around him that's given him such fast reflexes. I know I'd be moving as fast as I could to get away from all that conflict.*

I spent the day puttering around the apartment, enjoying the sense of being safe behind locks and wards.

As I ate my solitary supper, I realized I hadn't been over to check on Conor's cat since Wednesday. She couldn't have gone hungry – I'd left her a plentiful supply of kibble – but I owed her a can of tuna. And maybe I could get her to explain what Collum was the gateway for, if indeed that whole scene had been some sort of insight, and not just my brain making random dream-state associations.

I debated over the thumb drives. Would the one with the data on it be safer here, locked behind my wards? Or would it be safer on me? Earlier I'd thought it would be better to lock up the decoy, but now I wasn't so sure. If I had the real one on me and the bad guys caught me, I'd have nothing to bargain for my life with. But if the bad guys got in and got nothing but the fake for their trouble, at least they wouldn't have the info – but they'd come after me for sure.

And now there was another variable that hadn't been in play before yesterday: the cops knew who I was. If they were in bed with Drake's goons, would Drake have more of an incentive to kidnap me, or less? "Missing/dead actor" would be a more lurid headline, certainly, and my notoriety might discourage the bad guys from hurting me if they wanted the project to stay hush-hush.

But maybe they didn't care about keeping it quiet.

This was starting to remind me of the scene in *The Princess Bride* where Vizzini and the Dread Pirate Roberts argued over which riddle answer was the most logical.

In the end, I flipped a coin. "Heads, I leave the real one here. Tails, I keep it with me."

The first flip came up tails. I debated about whether to make it two out of three, then shrugged. This could go on all night. I pocketed the tuna and the thumb drive with the goods on it, grabbed my jacket, set my wards again, and headed off across town to Conor's place.

Dusk was falling as I got to the yellow-swathed arbor. I debated whether to take the tape down – it's not like the cops would find anything else of use in the house – but decided to leave the decision up to Collum.

Ducking under the tape, I called out to Tiger. "Here, kitty, kitty, kitty," I said sweetly, voice low. "I'm back, and I brought a surprise for you."

The ward-wall came down and the front door opened a crack. I strode in and shut the door. Immediately, as before, Tiger was all over me – rubbing against my legs and purring up a storm.

"Aw, did you miss me?" I said, bending over to scratch her between her ears.

Did you bring the…mmm…tuna? Oh, that feels nice…

Smirking, I said, "I *could* keep petting you. Or I could open the can I brought." I laughed as she bolted for the kitchen.

"So has anyone been by?" I asked while she gobbled.

Just Collum. He tried to coax me into a carrier. She snorted and went back to eating. *As if.*

"He's right, you know," I said. "You can't stay here forever. Conor's not coming back."

And Collum won't leave that enchanted cottage of his. I know. But give me some time. I'm still in mourning.

"What do you mean, 'enchanted cottage'?"

She shrugged. *It's just a turn of phrase. That's what Conor called it.*

"Because I had a dream last night, and in my dream, you told me Conor was the gate."

Gate to what?

"I was hoping you knew."

She snorted again. *Nope. No idea.* She licked up the last shreds of tuna and raised her head, licking her chops. Then she sat back on her haunches and delicately washed her whiskers with a paw.

"Satisfied?"

That was good. Next time, get the white tuna.

"Albacore? But it's more expensive. And it has more mercury in it."

She gazed at me. *Is mercury good?*

"No! It's toxic. It's poison."

I know what toxic means. I just thought maybe you would get me some. Just this once.

"Did Conor buy it for you?"

No. Her eyes closed to slits.

"Of course not. Because he wanted to keep you safe."

And now he never will. She stalked off and crouched under the far corner of the dinette table.

I dropped to the floor and sat there cross-legged. "Hey," I said. "I'm sorry. I was being a jerk."

Yes, you were. She sighed. *But I suppose I can forgive you if you bring me more tuna.*

I gave her a gimlet stare of my own. I couldn't tell whether she was playing me intentionally or whether it came naturally to her. "Tell me something," I said. "Did Conor grow up out in the woods with Collum and their parents?"

Of course. Where else would he have lived? That house has been in the family for hundreds of years.

"But he moved away to go to college. And then he refused to move back. Why?" I'd assumed it was a *how do you keep them down on the farm now that they've seen Paree?* thing. But Tiger had said Conor called the old homestead the "enchanted cottage," and it didn't sound like a term of endearment. And then there was my dream.

He wanted to live in the wider world. He told me he wanted to give back to the Earth in other ways than family tradition would allow him to.

"And family tradition involves…?" I thought for a moment. "What does Collum *do*, exactly?"

He carries on the family tradition. She was watching me intently, her pupils dilated.

"You're not answering my question."

You're right.

I tried it another way. "Did you ever live in the enchanted cottage?"

The tip of her tail twitched. *How could I? I'm only five.*

70

"And Conor's been gone from home for a lot longer. Gotcha. Have you been there, though?"

Nope. Her tail twitched again, more insistently.

"So you couldn't tell me whether it's enchanted or not, huh?"

Silence, other than more tail twitching.

I changed course a little bit. "Are Conor's parents still alive?"

Yes, but they're not here.

Collum had said much the same thing. "Where are they, then?"

They've emigrated to Ireland.

I remembered then that Collum had said he had family there. I hadn't realized he'd meant his parents. "That's interesting. Any particular reason why?"

Her tail stilled. *Ask Collum. I've said too much already.*

"Oho! Family secrets, huh? That's never good." I looked around, and my eyes fell on a shoelace on the floor at the base of the kitchen island. I stretched out and retrieved it, then sat up again and began dragging the shoelace back and forth along the floor. "I bet I know a secret about you."

Her eyes grew enormous. The closer the shoelace end got to her, the more focused on it she became – until at last, with a wiggle of her butt to set her back paws in position, she launched herself at her prey. She would have caught it, too, if I hadn't seen the butt wiggle. That gave me enough warning to pull the string away at the last minute. I laughed when she missed. She set herself in attack position again. On and on this went, until she dropped to the floor and refused to run again. Instead, she pawed at the shoelace as I dangled it over her. At last, she got up and scooted away.

I dropped the shoelace and announced my intention to scoop her litter box. She had no objection. I dropped the bag full of used litter in the trash, and took the opportunity to clean out Conor's refrigerator. Then I put the trash out and, with more head and chin scratches, bid Tiger goodnight.

Bring more tuna tomorrow!

"How do you feel about salmon?"

71

Her ears perked up. *I've never had salmon. Is it tasty?*

"You might like it. I'll bring some tomorrow."

And tuna, too. In case I don't like the salmon.

"Yes, ma'am." I let myself out, stepped past Tiger's wards – and came face to face with Allen Owings for the second time that day.

"Ah, Regina," he said. "Or is it Raney?"

"Hello, Allen. Are you here to do an exposé on the TV star who found a dead guy in the river?"

He glanced at Conor's house, where the lights had just gone out. "Maybe. Although right now, I'm more interested in what you were doing at a crime scene." He indicated the yellow tape.

"The owner is missing. I was feeding his cat."

His eyes narrowed. "And how do you know he's missing, let alone that he has a cat that needs feeding?" He shook his head. "Never mind. First, tell me how you got in."

"With the key under the mat, of course." I let my eyes go wide. "You mean it didn't occur to you to check for a key? Really, Allen, you need to work on your investigative skills."

"I *would* have checked," he said, his teeth set, "but I couldn't get near the place. How did you...?"

I shrugged. "I guess the cat likes me. Goodnight, Allen." I passed him and began to walk away.

"Happy to give you a lift," he called.

"Thanks, but no," I called back, and kept walking. I half expected him to follow and harass me until I agreed to get in his car, but he didn't.

Maybe he thought he could sweet-talk the cat into letting him in. *Good luck with that, buddy. You're not her type.*

Whatever her type might be. Gnomish geologist, I supposed.

And then I began to wonder how dumb Allen could possibly be. Here in the tiny town of Harpers Ferry, where nothing momentous had happened since the Civil War, all of a sudden the police were working two crimes at once: the drowning death of a John Doe and the disappearance of a local man. It wouldn't take a genius to wonder whether they were the same guy. Why hadn't Allen put two and two together yet? Our writers would have settled such an obvious clue in the first ten minutes of the show, not saved it for the Big Reveal.

Or maybe they *would* save it. The quality of writing on our show had definitely been going downhill. We'd all noticed it. It was like the showrunners had milked the idea for all it was worth in seasons one through three, and were now running on fumes. I knew some of the crew were taking bets on whether we'd be optioned for next year.

My agent had even cautioned me about taking this break. "You never know, Raney," he'd said. "You drop out of sight like this and people will forget your name. If your show gets axed while you're gone, you may have trouble finding another gig."

"Sid, seriously, don't worry about it," I'd told him. "It'll all work out. And I really need to get out of town for a while."

And I had, because I knew the ex-boyfriend was an egomaniac. As soon as I dropped out of sight, he'd gaze in his mirror and fall in love with his own reflection again, and all thoughts of getting revenge on me for dumping him would vanish. It was the only way I could think of to protect Mam.

Anyway, Allen was either seriously stupid, or he thought I knew everything and he planned to just follow me around until I cracked under the strain.

That merry thought sustained me until I got back to the Airbnb. Not only had my wards held, they hadn't been tried. Maybe it had been Allen who'd thrown the brick.

As I got into bed, it occurred to me that I hadn't heard from my international gnome of mystery in a couple of days. Instantly, my lower lip trembled and my eyes filled with tears. Sure, we'd only been together for one night, but I thought we'd had chemistry. I thought we had something to build on. Maybe I'd read too much into it? Or maybe I'd come on too strong before he left. He said he was a loner, but maybe that was his way of blowing me off. Maybe I was more into him than he was into me.

The worst part was that I had no way to contact him – no phone number, no email address, nothing. I was dead certain that I'd never be able to find his house again. Not on my own, anyway.

I sniffed hard and wiped my eyes. Then I reminded myself that I had a breakfast date with Rufus MacKay. If past experience was any guide, I'd run into Collum while I was out gallivanting with Rufus. *That* interaction would tell me all I needed to know.

CHAPTER 9 – SATURDAY

It took me longer to get to the diner than I'd expected. I'd once again done the logic dance with myself over which thumb drive to take, and it had sucked up more time than I'd thought it would. This time, Barney's Greatest Hits held pride-of-place on my keyring; I'd shoved the live drive into a smelly sock in my laundry bag.

Rufus, tall and flame-haired as he was, was easy to spot. He hadn't waited for me to snag a booth, which was good because the place was jammed. He waved me over and motioned to the seat across from him.

"I wasn't sure you'd show," he said as I settled in. "Coffee?"

"Please," I said, and he poured me a cup from the carafe on the table. "You really thought I'd ghost you? Why?"

"Because you're such a big deal. You're in the paper, Ms. Meadows." He shoved that morning's edition of the *Sentinel* toward me. Sure enough, there I was: *TV Star Identified as Finder of Kayaker's Body*, it said, and was accompanied by a stock photo of me at a movie premiere the previous winter. I remembered the event – the movie was terrible – and I was grateful to whichever photo editor had cropped out the ex, who had been standing next to me in the original shot.

Allen Owings had done a pretty good job with the write-up. He regurgitated our conversation from the day I found Conor's body, and then recapped my screen credits. I knew he'd pulled the info from Wikipedia because a couple of the details were wrong. No matter how often Sid got them fixed, some stupid fan would go in and change them back.

If anybody ever asks you, my stage debut was *not* as the front half of Rudolph the Red-Nosed Reindeer in my third-grade class's holiday pageant. I was the back half.

Why people would want to change that, I have no idea. The truth is so much funnier.

Anyway, I pushed the paper back and said, "Good thing I left that dress at home. Everybody in the diner would be staring at me otherwise." I grinned at him.

He smiled back. "You're not what I expected at all."

"What did you expect? A prima donna?"

He shrugged. "Yeah. Maybe."

"Yeah, no. My mother beat that out of me early." I glanced up from the menu in a hurry. "Figuratively speaking. She never actually beat me."

"I'm sure you were a perfect child," he said. "So well-behaved that she would never have needed to beat you."

My lips quirked. "Let's go with that," I said. "So what's good here?"

"Pretty much everything," he said, and we discussed the menu for a moment. Eventually I settled on a plate of eggs, bacon and cheese grits. Grits are not typically my thing, but Rufus insisted I had to try them. He got his usual, or so he said: three eggs, bacon, sausage, and a stack of pancakes. "I'm a growing boy," he said with a grin.

"So tell me what we're doing today," I said while we waited for our food.

He leaned forward, all traces of humor gone. "As you know, Alex Drake is the local state representative. He's also dumb as a box of rocks. He inherited the family construction business from his father and is steadily running it into the ground." He scowled. "Big D, his father, treated his employees like shit, and Little D does the same thing. It's worked for a lot of years because the job market has been so horrible here. But things are getting better now, and the workers want to be treated better. So they want to unionize." He sat back and spread his hands. "I'm here to help."

"How's it going?"

He snorted. "Not too well. But that's typical. Drake's tried all the usual tricks: intimidation, harassment, firing the instigators."

"Isn't that illegal?"

"Sure. But it never stops them from trying."

"What does stop them?"

"Press coverage, sometimes. Getting the cops involved, sometimes. Sometimes the cops are in cahoots with management, though."

I lowered my voice. "Is that happening here?"

He nodded briefly as the waitress brought our food. Once she was gone, he said, "Yeah. They're all in it together – Drake, the cops, and the money behind Drake's political career." He dug in, talking between mouthfuls. "The big-money types around here love him. He's a businessman like they are, he's got plenty of his own money to sink into campaigning, and he does anything they tell him to do."

"Tell me about that," I said, stirring the melted cheese into my grits. "He's running for Congress?"

"Not yet. But the smart money says he'll announce shortly."

"What if…" I took a bite of grits and decided they were an acquired taste. "Let's say someone came to Drake with information that would upend one of his big projects."

Rufus paused and looked up at me. "They'd be dead."

"Like literally?"

"Are we talking about the leprechaun's brother?"

"Yeah."

He chewed thoughtfully. Then he gestured to my plate. "Your eggs are getting cold."

So was my appetite. I managed a few forkfuls and the bacon. Rufus ended up eating the grits. Then he paid the bill – "You can get the check next time" – and we went out to his car.

Once on the road, he said, "All right. What did Collum's brother know that got him killed?"

I took a breath. "Do you believe in magic?"

He rolled his eyes. "Of course. Who do you think you're talking to?"

I stared at him. "I don't know. Who are you?"

He glanced over at me. "Raney. Think. We're not all here by chance."

"And who's 'we'?"

"You and me. Gail. The leprechaun."

"He's a *gnome*," I said.

He waved a hand. "Whatever. The point is, we're all Elementals."

"And how do you know that for sure?"

"It doesn't take a genius to figure it out, if you know what to look for," he said. "You've told me twice now that Collum's a gnome – that's Earth. You knew the guy didn't drown, so you must be an undine – that's Water. And Gail has got to be a sylph. I've never met an Airier woman in my life."

"Neither have I," I admitted. "Which means you're…"

"My affinity is Fire," he confirmed.

"You're a salamander."

"Half, yeah. On my father's side."

I blinked. "Salamanders can mate with humans?"

He grinned. "It's a little-known fact. But yeah."

Briefly, I wondered about the mechanics. Then I forced myself to put off the contemplation until later. "I'm also a halfling. So is Collum."

"So is Gail, I imagine," he said with a snort. "Otherwise she'd have blown away by now."

"I had lunch with her the other day," I said. "I'm pretty sure she knew I was an undine. She was dropping Airy hints like mad. I guess I should have called her on it."

"It doesn't matter. It all unfolds when it's supposed to. That's how the Universe works."

I nodded. That was always the way it had worked for me.

"So Collum's brother," he prompted. I told him everything – about my conversation with Shenandoah, and about the cops visiting Conor's house the night before I found his body, and about the wight. I didn't tell him Collum and I had slept together. I didn't think it was germane – or not yet, anyhow.

Maybe never, if Collum didn't show up again. I began to get a little weepy, but sucked it back. *Focus on the guy you're with!*

"Collum didn't happen to tell you the name of this gateway falls, did he?' Rufus asked.

"Nope. Just that it was hidden, or hard to find. He also said it's beautiful there."

"Of course it is," Rufus muttered. "Anyway, we're here." He pulled off to the side of the road and killed the engine.

I looked around. We were in a wooded area that looked very much like all the other wooded areas we'd been driving through. "Where, exactly, are we?"

"Oh, well, I can't drive up to the entrance and ask them to let me in," he said. "Drake hates me. He's told the guards not to let me on his property. So we'll have to walk from here." He checked the side mirror and opened his door. Then he looked over at me. "Got your hiking boots on?"

I glanced down at my sneakers. "No, but these should do," I said.

"They'll have to," he said, and got out of the car.

I shrugged, grabbed my daypack, and followed him.

It was shaping up to be another hot, muggy day. I was glad I'd thought to bring bug spray – the woods we walked through were teeming with mosquitoes. I sprayed myself and offered the bottle to Rufus, but he shook his head. "They don't bother me," he said. "Maybe I smell like a bug zapper to them."

"Must be nice. They love me." I stowed the bottle back in my pack.

He smirked. "Of course they do. Mosquitoes lay their eggs in water."

If I thought about that for too long, I'd start freaking out. "Lead the way," I said.

We hadn't walked far – half a mile, maybe – when we came to the edge of the woods. Beyond lay the Shenandoah River, and between it and us was a fenced construction site. A number of vinyl banners – the kind contractors use to boast they're working on a project – were tied to the fence at the far end of the site, near the gate, and the biggest one prominently featured a duck's head. A section of fence near us had pulled free of the post and bottom rail, leaving a hole big enough to crawl through.

Rufus held out an arm to block my path, then put a finger to his lips. When I nodded, he went a few steps farther and took a surreptitious look around. Then he motioned me forward. We scrambled through the hole, then dashed across the open field to where a group of construction workers were taking a break. A couple of the guys had doffed their hard hats; one of them was pouring water over his head and bare shoulders. Three or four were smoking cigarettes. The rest stood or sat, talking.

"Hey, Rufus," one of them said. "How'd you get here? The boss is gonna kick your ass out if he sees you."

"So he's not gonna see me," Rufus said. "This is Agnes. She's a friend of mine. She wanted to see what you guys are up against."

"Hey, Agnes, are you with the union?" one of the smokers said.

"Yeah, she is," Rufus said. "Where's Farmington? I need to talk to him."

"*Se ha ido*," one of the men said.

Rufus's brow lowered. "What do you mean, he's gone?"

"He got hurt," said another man in a heavy Hispanic accent.

Rufus's face and neck turned red. "How?"

The men shared a look. "Load of pipe fell on him," another guy volunteered. "Boss said it wasn't tied down right."

"Do you guys believe that?" Rufus asked.

Heads shook all around.

"God *damn* it," Rufus said. "Where's the boss?"

"He'll throw you out," said the first man who had spoken.

"I'm not gonna give him the chance. Where is he?"

A couple of the guys pointed to a trailer that sat off to one side of the site. I guessed it served as an office.

"C'mon," Rufus said to me, and we began walking toward the trailer.

"Come back, Agnes!" someone called. "You'll have more fun with me!" Laughter rang out, along with catcalls and kissing noises.

"Charming," I muttered.

"They're assholes," said Rufus. "But they deserve decent pay and safe working conditions." The tips of his ears were crimson.

We climbed the metal stairs to the office door and Rufus yanked it open. "Who's in charge here?" he bellowed.

"I am." The man who responded was just as tall as Rufus and twice his width. "What the fuck are you doing here, MacKay? This is private property! Get out!"

"Where's Farmington?"

The supervisor approached us. "I said, get out."

"Gonzalez says he got hurt," Rufus went on. "Something about a load of pipe not tied down properly. You know anything about that?"

"It was an accident!"

Rufus growled, "You can prove that, huh? You *know* it's illegal for the company to interfere with unionization efforts, Cass. Farmington was one of the biggest union supporters. How fucking convenient that he's now out of the way."

"Get the fuck out of here!" Cass bellowed.

"Watch your fucking mouth!" Rufus bellowed right back. "There's a lady present!"

His glance at me barely broke his stride. "Who's this? Is she with you?"

"I'm Agnes Thermopylae," I said, giving him my most charming smile.

"Well, Miss Thermopylae," Cass said, "you can get the fuck out of here, too. I'm calling the cops on you both." He reached into his pants pocket and pulled out a cell phone.

Rufus snatched the phone from his hand. His own hand glowed white-hot for a moment. Then he opened it and a melted blob of fused plastic and electronics dropped to the floor in front of Cass.

"You son of a bitch!" Cass screamed. "I just bought that phone!"

"I hope it was insured," I said sweetly.

Cass's face turned purple. Rufus grabbed my hand and we fled the trailer, with Cass rattling down the stairs after us, yelling, "Get out get out get out!"

The workers' cheers followed us as we dashed back into the woods. We didn't stop running until we got to the car. Rufus did a U-turn while I was still buckling in. The tires squealed as he hit the gas to get us out of there.

My heart was hammering. I looked at Rufus, sure he was as afraid as I was. But no – he was grinning from ear to ear. "Whoo hoo!" he yelled.

"How many times have you done that?" I asked.

"This was the first," he said. "And boy! It felt good!" He pounded the steering wheel. "That cocksucker has been a pain in my ass since the first day I got here!"

"Well, congratulations," I said. "What happens now?"

He sobered. "Now I need to figure out where Farmington is. They may have taken him to the hospital in Charles Town, but I'm guessing either Martinsburg or Winchester, depending on how badly he was hurt. Probably Martinsburg."

"Are you planning to just drive around, or…?"

He looked at me. "Nah. I'll go back to my hotel and make some calls. I need to call my boss, too. If this so-called accident played out the way I think it did, we'll be filing a lawsuit against Hookbill Inc. We'll get justice that way, since the cops refuse to uphold the law."

That reminded me of something I hadn't told him. "The cops searched Conor's house last Saturday," I said. "The day before I found his body."

He glanced at me in surprise. "They did?"

"They did. And they didn't put up the crime scene tape until the next day, after his body turned up."

"What were they looking for, I wonder?" he asked.

I fingered Barney's Greatest Hits in the pocket of my shorts. "I have no idea."

Rufus shot me a dubious look, but he let it go. "I'm sorry to cut this outing short, Raney, but I have a lot of work ahead of me. Can I drop you somewhere?"

"I'd appreciate it," I said, and gave him the address of the Airbnb. I was relieved that he didn't expect me to spend the rest of the day trailing after him.

As we pulled onto my street, I saw someone sitting on the steps leading to my front door. "Who is that?" I wondered aloud.

We identified my visitor at the same moment, but Rufus got it out first. "It's the leprechaun," he said, as my heart did a little flip.

He pulled to the curb and stopped. I opened the door and got out. "Thanks for breakfast, Rufus," I said. "And thanks for an exciting morning."

"Any time," he said with a grin. Then he cocked his head. "Well, hello there – Collum, is it?"

Collum had come up behind me. "Yeah. Hi, Rufus. Nice to see you again."

"Actually," Rufus said, "I'm glad you're here." He shut off the engine and got out of the car. "I don't have but a minute, but we need to talk."

Collum eyed him suspiciously. "About what?"

"About this gathering of Elementals," Rufus said. "You, me, Raney here, and Gail."

Collum's expression went blank. "Lead on," he said to me, gesturing toward my door.

"Not there," I said, suddenly wondering whether the apartment was bugged – and a fine time to think of it now. "Let's go around back. We can sit in the shade and talk."

Collum threw me an odd look, but Rufus shrugged and preceded us to the sidewalk that led to the back of the house.

There were, in fact, a table and chairs here in the shade – although the difference in temperature between the shade and full sun seemed negligible. Rufus pulled one of the chairs away from the table and sprawled in it. I sat in the one next to his, and Collum drew a third chair close to mine.

Rufus looked at the two of us, and sat up straighter. "Okay, for starters," he said, "I have no interest in your girl."

Collum's eyebrows rose.

"I'm not really…" I began. "I mean, we're…"

"Right. Sure. Whatever." Rufus ducked his head and waved one hand in the air. "Just wanted to put that out there."

I sucked in a breath. "Okay! Good to know."

"How much has she told you?" Collum asked. It seemed to me that he'd relaxed a bit.

As Rufus recapped what he knew, Collum nodded. Then he looked at me. "You didn't tell him about the thumb drive."

"Not yet, no."

"Where is it?"

I grinned. "I've been moving it around."

"No. I mean, do you have it with you? Because somebody messed with your wards this morning."

"What?" I stood in a hurry and went to the back door. Sure enough, someone had tried to jimmy my magical locks. Rapidly, I circled the house, checking to see whether anyone had managed to get in, but it didn't look like anyone had.

"Nice job of warding, by the way," Collum said, standing at my elbow, as I got to the kitchen door. He nodded at the scratched paint on the windowsill. "That's old, isn't it?"

"By a couple of days, yeah. That was an amateur." I toed the loose brick in the flower bed edging. "When the crowbar didn't work, he tried to break a window."

"Today, though, it wasn't an amateur," Rufus said.

"No," I said. "No, it wasn't. And I don't know who it might have been."

The three of us stood in silence for a moment. Collum began rubbing my back. I slipped my arm around his waist and leaned in.

Rufus gave us a sideways look. Then he said, "Look, I have stuff to do. Let's meet up for dinner tomorrow night at the Private Ensign. I'll take care of contacting Gail."

"Sounds good to me," I said, looking at Collum.

He looked down for a minute. Then he nodded. "Okay. I guess the more minds we have working on this, the better."

We watched Rufus get in his car and drive away. Then I took down my wards and we went in the house.

"Do you want some tea?" I asked. "Or…"

Collum pulled me against him and kissed me deeply.

When we came up for air, I said, "I was gonna suggest lunch, but this is fine.'" He smiled, and his lips came down on mine again. I stretched my arms up and wrapped them around his neck. He fitted his hands to my butt and pulled me closer. I dropped my hands to the front of his jeans.

We were too far gone to make it to the bedroom. The sofa was not as comfortable, but it was more convenient.

"Well," I said, when we were both spent.

"I missed you," he said.

"I guess you did," I said with a laugh. Then my smile faded. "Listen, Collum. I need to have a way to contact you."

"Why?"

"Because there were a thousand times that I thought to myself, 'I need to remember to tell Collum this,' and now I've forgotten all of them."

"A thousand? Really?"

"Maybe not a thousand. But hundreds of times."

"Hundreds is a lot." He planted kisses slowly down my neck.

"It is," I agreed.

85

"You taste so good," he said. "Like a cool drink of water." He captured my nipple with his lips and teased it with his tongue.

A sigh escaped me. "Are we gonna do this again already?"

"No time like the present," he said, and reached lower.

Many minutes later, he said, "Now I'm hungry."

I laughed at him. "I could cook something. Or we could order in."

He nodded. "Those are the typical choices." He glanced at me. "Or I could cook you something."

"You can cook? You're a man of many talents," I said, tracing circles on his stomach.

We lay there, pressed together on the sofa, for another few minutes. Then he sighed. "If we don't get dressed, we'll never eat."

"I'm okay here for a while yet. You're the one who's hungry."

He sat up and maneuvered to one end of the sofa. I scooted around and tucked my feet under me.

"It was really hard for me to leave the other night," he said. "Really hard."

"You could have stayed," I said.

"I know. But…" He leaned forward and put his forearms on his knees. "I've just been at this for so long on my own."

I frowned. "I'm not sure what you mean."

He looked up at me. "I have certain things I'm responsible for. Things I need to keep watch over every day. I just can't be away for too long. I don't know what would happen if…"

I was still in the dark. "Are we talking about you staying over, or something else?"

He raised his hands and dropped them again. "This idea of us all getting together and fighting whatever it is. I feel like if we do that, it'll mean I'm a failure." He looked up at me again. "I don't think I'm explaining myself very well."

"No, I think I get it," I said slowly. "If you need help, it feels like you're a failure."

He nodded and stared at the floor. "Yeah."

"Well, you're not," I said, putting a hand on his shoulder. I still didn't know exactly what he was talking about, but I dropped my shielding, for lack of a better term, and let my emotions respond to his. "The job's just gotten bigger, that's all, in ways you never anticipated. There's no shame in asking for help."

"Conor should be helping," he muttered, and covered his eyes with one hand.

"I know you miss him," I said, rubbing slow circles on his back. "But he did help, didn't he? He did what he could, and it just wasn't enough. He was up against something that was too strong for him. Stronger than he realized."

"Too strong," he echoed.

"Not for all of us together." I leaned over and kissed his cheek. "You're doing the right thing by letting us help. I don't think you're a failure. I think you're strongest when you can admit you're in over your head."

He turned to look at me. "Really?"

"Really. Generals call for reinforcements all the time when they're overwhelmed."

"You don't think I'm a failure?"

I turned his face to mine. "I think you're wonderful."

His expression softened and gladness shone from his eyes as he reached for me.

It was the sweetest kiss I'd ever received.

He chuckled and wiped a tear away with his thumb. "You're not melting, are you?"

"No, it's just..." I laughed softly. "My emotions get too big for me sometimes."

He kissed me. Then he sighed. "Lunch. Right."

"Right." I got up and reached for my shorts. "I still need a way to get messages to you, mister."

He sighed. "See, I don't have a cell phone. Coverage isn't very good at home."

"But I needed you." My emotional defenses were still down – otherwise I might not have admitted that, or not this early in the relationship. "I missed you so much. I didn't know what was going on – whether I'd read the situation wrong or done something to upset you or..."

"No, it was nothing like that," he said, enfolding me in his arms. "It was all me." He added bitterly, "And this stupid job I have to do."

"We're gonna fix that," I said, looking up at him. "Tomorrow. And then you're going to get a phone. For me."

He laughed. "Okay. For you."

I raised up on my toes and kissed him. Then, "Lunch," I said.

"Lunch. Right."

He looked through my supplies and whipped together a tasty combination I never would have thought to make. I decided I could get used to dating a guy who could cook.

CHAPTER 10 – SUNDAY

Collum still couldn't stay all night, but I felt confident we were working that out. So I didn't puddle up too badly when we said goodbye.

It was pretty late when he left, though, and so it was pretty late when I woke up. I had to rush through my morning routine to be at the Private Ensign by the appointed time. I did not, however, forget to reset the wards as I left – even though I was carrying the good stuff this time. However, I left the decoy sitting out in plain sight on the coffee table. If by some miracle my would-be intruder managed to get in while I was gone, I didn't want him tearing up the place to find what he was looking for.

The Private Ensign was empty when I arrived, but the black bouncer with the fathomless eyes was working the door. "Good to see you again," he said.

"Do you guys do a brunch menu on Sundays?" I asked.

"I can get you anything you want," he said, handing back my I.D. Somehow I got the feeling he meant more than food or drinks. I smiled weakly and went in.

When I say the place was empty, I mean it was *empty*. No waitress, no bartender, no cooking smells wafting out from the kitchen. Just a fire burning low in the fireplace, giving off light without heat, and a table set for four. Well, that's not entirely true. I noticed some furnishings I'd never seen before: a fountain had sprung up on the wall to the right of the fireplace; a set of wind chimes hung from the ceiling near the entry foyer, across from the fountain; and a tree had apparently taken root in the floor across from the fire.

I blinked and looked again. The fireplace had always been on the south wall, and Element of South was Fire. I realized that my subconscious self had noted the location of the fireplace when I first walked in, and it had gone a long way toward making me feel at home immediately.

These new additions had been oriented at their correct compass points: The wind chimes were Air, and hung in the East; the fountain was Water, and bubbled in the West; and the sapling, representing Earth, grew in the North. The table for four had been placed in the very center of the room.

In short, someone had gone to a great deal of trouble to make the Private Ensign into a ritual space.

I grew uneasy. Elementals have magic, but it's inherent in us. It's not the sort of magic that a wizard could steal, or even channel, for his own purposes. We are the living embodiment of the Elements. We can't give our power away. That's why most of us spend most of our lives hiding our powers from humankind – because even though we can't give our power away, or have it stolen from us, it doesn't stop nefarious individuals from trying. It's just a lot healthier for everyone involved if the greedy and power-hungry have no idea who we are.

I prepared to beat a retreat. But as I turned, I ran into Gail, who was just coming in. "Oh!" she cried, upon seeing the restaurant's makeover. "Isn't this lovely!"

"Yeah," I said. "Lovely. Listen, Gail, I just realized I left something at home."

"Can't you fetch it later?" That was Rufus, who followed Gail in. The two of them made a slow circuit of the room, starting in the East where we'd all come in and progressing sunwise.

"Um, guys?" I said. "Doesn't this seem a bit contrived to you?"

"Not at all!" said Gail. "I think it's a sweet tribute to us. It's obvious the owners know who and what we are."

"That's what worries me," I said.

I heard an intake of breath, and turned to the entryway. There stood Collum, his mouth agape as he took in the room's furnishings. "Uh," he said.

"Yeah," I agreed. "This is giving me the creeps. Can't we meet somewhere else, you guys?"

Rufus had found his seat and was taking a swig of the beer sitting at his place as I spoke. He froze for a moment. Then he swallowed and put down his mug. "I wish you'd said that a minute ago. Now I'm going to have to settle up before we leave," he said.

"Oh, let's stay," said Gail, taking her seat. "We're all here together. What can they do to us? It's not like we're helpless."

I thought of Mam, who was most assuredly not helpless, but who would die an untimely and agonizing death if my father ever found her. "I'm not sure that's enough to protect us," I said.

Collum, meanwhile, had been studying the oak tree. "It's definitely real," he murmured, catching a leaf between his thumb and forefinger. The chimes rang wildly, the fire billowed in the grate, and the fountain became a miniature cataract. He looked around with wide eyes and let go of the leaf. At once, everything subsided.

"Magic," I said. I made my own circuit of the room and stopped before the fountain. It was the kind you set on a tabletop to help with a room's feng shui. But those always have a tiny pump with a motor and a battery pack or power plug, and this had neither one. I stuck my finger in the water, just in case it was a projection or something. Unlike when Collum pinched the oak leaf, my action didn't stir anything up. Maybe the tree had thought he would pick the leaf.

I put my wet finger in my mouth. The water tasted pure and sweet.

"Good?" Collum asked, leaning over to inspect my finger.

"Yeah," I said. He smiled, and arm in arm, we promenaded past the fire and chimes.

Then we took our seats. "I'm willing to stick around to see what happens next," Collum said.

"Okay," I said. "I just hope we don't regret it."

My butt hitting the chair must have been a signal. Here came the bouncer, menus under one arm. "Welcome to the Private Ensign," he said with a smile that bordered on glee. "We're so happy you're here with us."

"Who's 'us'?" I asked.

"All will become clear. Please, take your time with your menu," he said as he passed them out. "I'll be right here when you're ready." And he meandered away, toward the darkened kitchen.

"You think he's going to cook our orders, too?" I asked.

"Shh," Collum said. "Take a look."

I glanced at my menu. Then I looked again. There was only one thing on it: fried catfish. "There must be some mistake," I said. "This isn't the regular menu. And I don't eat fish." *Some of them are my friends.*

"Where do you see fish?" asked Rufus. "The only thing on mine is blackened lizard."

"All I have is roast quail," said Gail, puzzled. "I don't eat quail."

"Collum?" I asked. "What's on your menu?"

His lips were trembling. "This is some kind of sick joke," he said, shoving his menu at me. The only option on it was charcoal-grilled wight.

I raised my hand with Collum's menu in it. "Waiter," I called. "There's been some kind of mixup."

Instantly he appeared, laden with four identical plates covered with identical silver domes. "I'm terribly sorry," he said smoothly. "Here you are." He set a plate down before each of us and bustled away.

We looked at each other. "On the count of three," I said. "One, two, three…" In unison, we lifted our covers and sighed with relief. Our plates held nothing weirder than the Private Ensign's house burger with steak fries.

"This has been a very strange meal so far," Gail said as we dug in. "I'm a little leery of beginning our discussion here."

"I hear you," Rufus said. "But I don't think we have any time to waste." He swirled a fry in ketchup and popped it in his mouth. "Raney, I tracked down Farmington."

"Oh? Which hospital did they take him to?"

"Winchester. And it's not looking good. Three broken ribs and a shattered pelvis."

Collum shook his head. "Poor guy."

"It'll be months before he can work again," Rufus went on. "Of course Drake is too cheap to provide sick leave or insurance, so he'll probably be fired. His wife doesn't make enough money to support the family by herself, let alone pay a big hospital bill." He was getting angrier, the longer he spoke. "Someone needs to teach Drake a lesson. He can't do that to people."

"Agreed," Collum said. "He can't just kill people and dump them in the river, either."

Rufus put a hand on Collum's forearm and squeezed. Collum nodded his thanks. When Rufus removed his hand, it looked to me like Collum's sleeve was smoking. But then Gail breathed out and the smoke wafted away.

"So what do we do?" I said. "Do we go back to the construction site?"

Rufus shook his head. "Drake's never there. We need to confront him at his office."

"Where's that?" I asked.

"Up on Schoolhouse Ridge, near the river."

Collum whistled low. "That's some nice real estate up there."

"He's got a killer view of the river and the mountains," Rufus said. "And it's not too far from Lost Falls." He eyed Collum as he spoke.

Collum nearly choked on his burger. He chewed deliberately, swallowed, and then turned to Rufus. "What do you know about Lost Falls?"

"Raney happened to mention there was a beautiful waterfall near this site where your family sequestered the wight, whenever it was," Rufus said. "I did some digging and put two and two together."

"Wait, wait, wait," Gail said, waving one hand while she dabbed a napkin to her lips with the other. "What wight?"

Collum was looking daggers at me. I gave him a guilty smile. "It was all going to come out eventually," I said.

"As it has," he said, none too pleased.

"Spill it, leprechaun," Gail said sharply.

"He's not a leprechaun," I said.

Collum put up both hands to stop us. "Ladies, please," he said. "It's all right, Raney. It's not the first time I've been on the receiving end of an insult."

Gail straightened. "My apologies, Collum. It's just that Rufus always calls you that. I didn't realize he was causing trouble."

"I'm not," he said, laughing. "They're the same thing."

"No, they're not," said Collum evenly.

"Functionally," Rufus said.

"No. They're. Not." Collum closed his eyes and took a breath. "They do both live underground. But Gnomes are Earth Elementals. Leprechauns are what's left of the Tuatha de Danaan, the ancient kings of Ireland."

"The Tuatha were gods," Gail said.

"They were," Collum confirmed. "They're not anymore."

"That's right," said Rufus. "Now all they do is guard their pots of gold and whack people over the head with their shillelaghs." He grinned slyly and put on a fake Irish accent. "And I'm not after insulting yer man here because he isn't one. Am I right, me boyo?"

"Just stop," I said. "If we're going to work together, we need to get along."

Rufus sighed and ducked his head. "Oh, all right. I was just having a little fun. Sorry, Collum."

"Accepted." Then a slow smile crept across Collum's face. "You stop calling me a leprechaun, and I won't ask you any pointed questions about your lizard brain."

"Here, now," said Rufus, turning pink.

"Boys!" I cried. "I said stop it. We have to come up with a game plan, but we're never going to get it done if you two keep bickering!"

The guys grinned at each other. And now I felt like an idiot. They'd been doing the male bonding thing and I'd misinterpreted it.

Gail cleared her throat. "Have we settled everything? Apologies accepted all around?" Hearing no objections, she said. "Good. Thank you. Now then, Collum – you were about to explain to us about this wight of yours."

"It's not mine," he said. Then he launched into the explanation he'd given me: How, centuries ago, his people had essentially trapped the wight between worlds by setting it to guard the last major coal seam in West Virginia. "The gate," he said with a nod to Rufus, "is indeed at Lost Falls. And somehow Drake found out about it. What my brother discovered was that Drake plans to blow up the mountain to get to the coal."

"And that will release the wight," Gail said. "Got it. I think I'm up to speed now."

"Conor and I had dinner together the Wednesday before he disappeared," Collum said. "He told me Drake's project could not be allowed to go on – but he didn't tell me why. He planned to confront Drake the next day. I never saw him again." His gaze unfocused for a moment. "On Sunday, I felt prompted to go down to the A.T. where it parallels the Shenandoah River. That's when I met Raney." He nodded at me. "She'd found Conor's body just a few hours before."

"I already knew that Conor didn't die by drowning," I told them.

"Right," said Gail. "You said he didn't have any water in his lungs."

"Right. And then there's this," I went on. "Conor's cat told me there were two groups of men who searched the house after Conor left for the last time. The first group was Thursday night. We assume they were Drake's men." I cut a look at Collum. "Then the police came through on Saturday."

"Saturday!" Collum said. "You never told me that."

"I kept getting distracted," I said sheepishly. "Sorry. But yeah, that's what Tiger said."

"What were these goons looking for?" Gail asked.

In response, I pulled my keyring from my pocket and dangled it for all to see. "The plans for the destruction of Lost Falls," I said.

Collum looked hard at the thumb drive attached to my keys, but said nothing.

"They know I have this," I said. "I think they do, anyway. There have been a couple of attempts to break into the place where I'm staying."

Rufus's mind was running along another track. "So here's what I think happened," he said. "Conor went to see Drake at his office on Thursday. They argued, and somehow Conor was killed. I'm thinking it was deliberate, not accidental. Conor simply knew too much about what was going on." He glanced at Collum. "Sorry, dude."

"It's okay," he said, although his eyes were red-rimmed. "Go on."

"They had to get rid of the body," Rufus resumed. "So they came up with this lame story about a missing kayaker. What day did the empty kayak turn up?"

"Thursday," Gail said. "It was Thursday. I remember because I was volunteering in the visitor center when the news came in. I always volunteer on Wednesdays and Thursdays," she told me.

"Thursday," Rufus echoed. "So they threw the body in the river and then cobbled together their alibi. And got the cops in on it."

"And the medical examiner," I said. "To fake the cause of death. I wonder what Conor actually died of?"

"It would be helpful to know," Collum rumbled. "Then we'd have a better idea of what, or who, we're up against."

Rufus looked at him with interest. "You think Drake had Otherworldly help?"

Collum pushed his empty plate away. "He had to," he said. "That gateway was hidden with Earth power, and the shielding is renewed at every new moon. With. Out. Fail." He slapped the table to emphasize each syllable. "No mortal could have discovered it alone."

"Who renews it?" I asked.

He paused. For a moment, his lower lip trembled. Then he said, "I do."

Collum is *the gate*.

For a split second, I didn't know what to say – or rather, I didn't know how to respond without saying the wrong thing. Then my emotions staged a revolt. Automatically, I reached out to take one of his hands in both of mine. "Not anymore," I heard myself say. "You're not in this alone anymore."

"That's right," Gail declared. "We'll all help you. Won't we, Rufus?"

"Sure," he said. "All for one and one for all, and all that stuff. I'll do a ritual bloodletting at midnight every month, if it means Drake will get what's coming to him."

"Oh, he will," said Collum. He hadn't taken his eyes off me since I took his hand. "He will."

The scene around us changed. The Private Ensign faded away, and we were in a place I'd never seen before. The walls and floor were made of some kind of black rock – lava, maybe – or maybe they were just scorched. An odd burnt smell permeated the place. It wasn't sulfur, so I knew we weren't in Hell. And anyway, the directional markers had come with us, although altered: the tabletop fountain was now a freshwater cascade down a rock face, into a pool that glimmered in the light of the fireplace-turned-bonfire; the oak tree grew tall and strong; and the wind chimes were a pipe organ made of stalactites and sounded melodiously in every errant breeze.

Our table, too, was gone. We stood in the center of this cavernous space. And with us stood the African-American bouncer with the fathomless eyes.

"Who are you?" I asked, awed.

"My name in your world is Cassius Kimbell," he said, and gave us a radiant smile. "I have been waiting for you for a long, long time."

"This is Aether," said Gail, looking around.

"Yes," said Cassius.

"Why have you been waiting for us?" asked Rufus. It had the sound of a ritual question.

"An ancient evil has awakened," Cassius intoned.

"The wight," I said. "We know."

"No," he said. "The wight is not the evil. But the evil will awaken the wight." He turned to Collum and held his gaze. "This ancient power is too strong for one Elemental to fight alone. All the Elements must be joined together. Fused. Their purpose must be one purpose. Their powers separately are not strong enough to defeat this evil, but together their powers will expand exponentially. Only then will good prevail."

I looked around our little circle. "Does it matter that we're not all pure?" I asked. "I'm only half Elemental."

"So am I," said Collum.

"So am I," Rufus said.

"Me, too," Gail said.

Cassius smiled. "That is why we have waited for you. Your humanity is crucial. Mortals must be part of the solution."

That answered that. Kind of. But mortality brought its own responsibilities, and I was pretty sure – at least in my case – the world would notice if I suddenly became part of a four-person, uh, person. "So Cassius? How does this work, exactly? Because my show's only on hiatus. I need to go back to Hollywood soon and finish my scenes."

"Same," said Rufus, sounding nervous. "I mean, not the part about having a TV show. But I have a job to do in the mundane world, and I need to get back to it."

Gail shrugged and laughed. "I'm free as a bird."

To Cassius, our objections were inconsequential. "The sacrifice must be voluntary, or all is lost. Mankind will be lost. The Earth Herself will be lost."

Rufus swallowed. Then his expression hardened. "If this will bring down that bastard Alex Drake, I'm in," he said.

"I'm in," Gail echoed.

"I'll do whatever it takes to avenge my brother's death," said Collum quietly.

I gazed at him, my heart overflowing: sorrow for his losses; concern for the impossible tasks he must do each day; and yes, love. I wanted simultaneously to throw my arms around him to protect and support him, and go to pieces in the pool behind me. Neither of those, alas, would give the world what it needed to survive.

"Yes," I said, my mouth uncharacteristically dry. "I'm in, too."

Cassius raised his arms above his head, palms up, in the posture of supplication. "We are here in Aether," he cried, "where everything comes to be."

As he spoke, the flames of the bonfire leapt higher. The waterfall grew into a cataract. The cavern rumbled underfoot, setting the oak tree's branches thrashing and causing the chimes to produce tones of deep urgency.

Cassius didn't miss a beat. "These Elementals of Earth, Air, Fire, and Water come of their own free will to meet our greatest need. They would fight for this world. They *will* fight for this world. Let them become our champions!" Limned in green flames, he screamed, "Let them *become!*"

I felt odd, as if my life's essence was pouring from me. I looked down, and from the center of my chest I saw what looked to me to be a geyser of water of the purest blue. It rose above me in a graceful arc. I would have called it beautiful if I hadn't felt like I was dying.

Wildly, I looked around. Collum, too, had something pouring from his chest – a pillar of stone and leaves pressing skyward. His face was ashen.

Gail appeared to be in shock. A whirlwind protruded from her chest, and it also blew higher and higher.

Only Rufus seemed sanguine about what was happening to us – but the river of fire and blood emanating from *his* chest was the most frightening of all.

Cassius was still screaming his incantation, but he might have been speaking ancient Aramaic for all I could understand of it. All I knew was that my life was slipping away from me and toward something else.

Our arcs rose high above our heads. The light from Rufus's fire danced on the ceiling far above us, bathing the scene in crimson. In the last seconds before I became insensible, I realized our emanations were reaching for each other.

And just as I thought my next breath would be my last, they met.

The sound was deafening. The floor beneath us shuddered so violently that I would have been thrown to the ground had I not been fixed in place by our joining. Power flowed back down through my life's essence and revived me. The Earth, Air, and Fire of my friends sustained me, just as my Water sustained them.

Brimming with life, with power, with knowledge of all creation, I yelled for pure joy.

Then all at once, the connection snapped and I passed out.

CHAPTER 11 – NO TELLING WHAT DAY IT WAS

I came to on the floor of my own apartment. I was alone – not even Collum was with me. If I'd made it here under my own power, I had no recollection of it.

Shaking, I pulled my phone out of my pocket. It was the middle of Sunday afternoon. At least I hadn't missed a day.

I crawled on all fours to the bathroom, where I turned on the taps to the tub and tumbled in, clothes and all. I did have the presence of mind to empty my pockets first. But that was my last conscious thought before I gave myself to the water.

Hours later, I awoke, floating naked in the now-cold water in the tub.

I splashed upright and scrambled out. Then I sat, panting with fright, on the edge of the tub. My sodden clothing still floated freely at the other end, rippling in the wake I'd created with my sudden departure.

I crossed my arms over my breasts and shivered, wide-eyed. I had never spontaneously reassembled like that before.

But then I couldn't remember a time when I'd ever passed out in the water, either. Maybe the reassembly was a built-in failsafe?

It was an interesting theory, but I didn't care to test it just then.

From where I sat, I could just reach the edge of a bath towel hanging on the rack next to the sink. I pulled it down and wrapped it around my shoulders, then pushed my matted hair out of my eyes and thought.

I had a clear memory of everything that had happened in the crucible until I blacked out. After that, I recalled bits and pieces. I hadn't gotten home on my own, but no Otherworldly power had been involved – Cassius had helped us into his SUV and then took us home. I remembered being surprised at the size of Gail's house, and wondering what she had done for the government before she retired.

I was next to last to be dropped off. Collum was still in the car when Cassius pulled up outside my place. I'd managed to kiss Collum, then made a good show of getting up to the door under my own power. I must have dropped like a ton of bricks just inside the door.

The wards!

Panic gave me strength. Wrapping the towel clumsily around my torso, I dashed to the front door – and let out a sigh of relief. The wards were in place. I didn't remember redoing them once I'd gotten inside, but I…

No. These weren't mine. But they felt familiar. Safe. Like a lullaby.

"Mam?" I called to the open air.

She walked out of the kitchen, her hands wrapped around a steaming mug. "It's a good thing Cassius asked me to come," she said. "You shouldn't have left that door unwarded. You can't keep being so careless, Raney."

"I'd passed out!" I said, outraged. Somehow she always managed to make me feel like a five-year-old.

"It's all right, my dearest," she crooned, putting an arm around my shoulders. "Mam's here now. Everything's going to be just fine." She shoved the mug into my hand. "Have some tea. But you should get dressed first. You'll catch cold, running around like that."

I sat the mug on the coffee table and headed to the bedroom, where I hastily donned a t-shirt and my other pair of jeans. "You ought not to have come," I called as I made myself decent. "It's dangerous here. There's been a murder, and the gnomes have sequestered a land wight, and…wait." I pulled the t-shirt over my head and went back to the living room. "You know Cassius?"

"Not well," she said, leading the way to the kitchen.

I retrieved my tea and followed her. "But well enough for him to get word to you to come."

"More or less." She sat at the table and sipped, giving me an innocent look over the rim of her mug. Then she leaned forward. "How do you feel?"

"Fine," I said automatically. Then I thought about it. "Kind of more than fine. I guess I really needed that nap. The ritual took a lot out of me."

"And put a lot back into you," she said.

"What?"

"Go look in the mirror." Her tone held suppressed excitement.

I glared at her suspiciously – I assumed she was making some kind of obscure joke about my uncombed hair – and sprang out of my chair. I scooped up the keyring that was still lying on the bathroom floor in a fluid motion, grabbed the comb on the counter, and began to go at my snarls – and froze, comb in midair.

I looked different. The shape of my features hadn't changed and my hair was definitely still a mess, but I looked different. Red highlights had found their way into my dishwater blonde hair, and my eyes – which had always been a watery blue – had taken on flecks of green and yellow.

"Is this what they call hazel eyes?" I called to Mam.

She appeared in the doorway. "I believe so."

I turned this way and that, watching the overhead light play on my newly-tinted eyes. Then I thought about what the change might mean. I turned to Mam. "What else did I get from the others?"

She crossed her arms and waited for me to figure it out.

There was my newfound energy. I felt peppier than I ever had, and I'd been moving around the apartment a lot faster than usual. Was that a gift of Air or of Fire? Or both?

And what did I get from Earth?

I glanced at the tub where my clothes still floated. "Oh no," I said. "I haven't lost my oneness with Water, have I?"

"I don't believe so," said Mam. "Undines who join with other Elementals don't typically lose the ability, but they might have trouble maintaining it."

I nodded slowly. "That would explain why I woke up reassembled." I looked at her. "Did the others get some of my abilities, too?"

"Very likely. The transference is a four-way street."

"None of this is new to you," I said.

She shrugged. "I've heard of such joinings before, when times were difficult and Elementals were called on to work together. But usually it happens only in the most dire of circumstances." She cocked her head. "What did Cassius say about it?"

I turned back to the mirror to attack my hair again. "Nothing, really. I got more information from Shenandoah than we did out of Cassius." I winced as I hit a particularly tough knot, and worked at with both hands. "Both of them said an ancient evil has awakened, and Cassius said it's not just the land wight that the gnomes sequestered in the Otherworld." I succeeded in teasing out the knot, and combed that section of hair smooth. "But that's all I know." I looked at Mam's reflection in the mirror. "We need a lot more information."

Mam looked troubled. "Where do we find Cassius?"

"He's the bouncer at the Private Ensign. But other than tracking him down at work, I don't know how else to contact him." I put the comb down. "I don't know how to contact anybody, really. I mean, I think I have phone numbers for Gail and for Rufus, but I still don't know how to get hold of Collum in a pinch." I turned around and leaned against the vanity, bracing my hands on the counter. "Shouldn't we have a phone tree or a Facebook group or something?"

Mam laughed. "I thought Facebook was only for old people."

"You know what I mean." I opened my mouth to say more, but I thought I heard a whisper. "Did you hear that?"

"What?"

I held up one hand and listened again. "It sounded like someone calling my name." I shook my head.

"Maybe your phone tree is calling," she suggested.

I shot her a withering look, then put my finger to my lips and listened again.

I was right. Someone was calling my name. Then whoever it was knocked on the front door.

"Oh," I said, deflated. "Excuse me, Mam." And I went to answer the knock.

When I opened the door, there stood Allen Owings – and he was seething.

"Oh, hello, Allen," I said, blocking the door so he couldn't barge in.

"What do you know about an explosion at the Private Ensign?" he demanded. I must have turned white, because he crowed, "You know something! I just knew you had to be involved!" He pulled out his phone, set it to record, and said, "Tell me everything."

"Starting with...?" I asked mildly.

"The explosion at the Private Ensign!"

"There was an explosion at the Private Ensign? That's terrible! When was it? Was anyone hurt?"

"You tell me," he ground out. "You were seen leaving the scene of the crime."

"Crime?" I said. "How do you know it was a crime? Maybe it was a gas leak or something."

"The police say it was foul play," he informed me.

I'd had enough of these small town secrets. Time to set this moron straight. "Yeah, well, the police also said the guy I found in the Shenandoah drowned, but he didn't have any water in his lungs. Your medical examiner lied about that. The victim was already dead when his killers dumped him in the river. And the river god isn't happy they befouled his waters with the guy's blood."

Allen's mouth hung open. He closed it with an audible snap. "How can you possibly know..."

"You asked me at the press conference what I knew that you didn't," I went on. "Well, that's it. That's the thing I was holding out on you."

"The *river god?*" he spluttered. "What kind of idiot do you take me for?"

"Go ask the cops, if you don't believe me," I said.

He was shouting. "I'm asking *you* about the explosion at the Private Ensign!"

"There was no explosion," I said patiently. There couldn't have been; I didn't remember any sense of panic when we left the restaurant. "Go check it out. The building's not damaged and no one was hurt. There's no story here." I leaned out of the door toward him. "But there *is* a story they're not telling you about. It's about a dirty politician who has dirty cops in his back pocket so he can finish his dirty construction project."

"Alex Drake?" he asked, incredulous.

"One of his employees is in the hospital in Winchester with severe injuries from an on-the-job accident," I went on. "His name is Farmington. He was trying to unionize his fellow workers. Now he's laid up and he has no health insurance." My tone oozed sarcasm. "Maybe your newspaper could set up a GoFundMe to cover his expenses."

"Are you trying to tell me that Alex Drake had that kayaker killed?" he scoffed.

"Did you hear *anything* I just said? Anything at *all?*" I rolled my eyes so hard that I was surprised I didn't end up staring at the back of my head. "Look, I need to go. Nice chatting with you." And I closed the door.

"Wait!" he cried, shoving the toe of his shoe toward the crack. But my quickened reflexes left him in the dust. I left him pounding on the door and yelling my name, and went to rejoin Mam in the kitchen.

"Let's move to the living room," I suggested. "It'll be quieter there, in case Allen comes around to the side door."

"Good idea," she said, and picked up the pot. I followed her with our mugs. Once ensconced on opposite ends of the sofa, Mam freshened up our tea and we sat back to sip as if it were just another day.

"I really do need to figure out a way to get hold of everyone," I said. "We need to come up with a game plan." *And I'm dying to compare notes with*

106

the others to see what's happened to them. "Oh, wait. I know." I pulled my phone from my jeans pocket; there in "all calls" was Rufus's number. I hit redial, and only then remembered Mam. "Sorry, but this is important."

She waved away my concern. "Do what you need to do, my dear. I'll see about starting dinner."

"Good luck," I said ruefully. With a pang, I remembered the last person who had presided over this kitchen to cook a meal for me, and wished for the hundredth time that I had a phone number for him.

The line clicked. "Hullo?"

"Rufus!" My shoulders eased down from around my ears. "How are you?"

He groaned. "I've been better."

I tensed again. "Why? What happened? Did someone attack you?"

"Not unless you count Cassius in that cavern." He groaned again. "My head is splitting."

"Well, take some ibuprofen or something," I snapped. "We need to get the gang together and figure out a plan. The sooner, the better."

"The *gang?*" he chortled. "We need a name. The way you just said that made us sound like a bunch of thugs."

I laughed. "Maybe we *are* a bunch of thugs. Or we could pretend to be. We could get t-shirts that say *Elemental Thug Life.*"

"No."

"In cursive. With festive little flowers around the words."

"No."

"Come on, it'd be fun."

"*No.*" He was only playing the curmudgeon, I could tell.

I pretended to pout. "Spoilsport. I bet Gail will help me."

"Feel free to call her."

"I'm going to. Where should we meet and when?"

"I thought you were organizing this," he grumbled.

"It should be someplace where the cops won't think to look for us," I went on. "Or that reporter from the *Sentinel.* He was here a little while ago, asking me a bunch of dumb questions." I paused there. I figured the details of my conversation with Allen Owings could wait.

Rufus sighed. "All right, tell you what. Let's get together at Jefferson Rock. We can try to find Collum's place from there. I have an idea about how to get to it."

"Sounds good."

"But give me an hour. I need to get something to eat first — I'm starving."

CHAPTER 12 – SUNDAY EVENING

Gail was in, as I was sure she would be – although she was less enthusiastic about the t-shirt idea than I'd hoped. Maybe Collum would be on board.

I mean, he probably wouldn't be to start with. But I was pretty sure I could talk him around.

Jefferson Rock is a shale formation just off the Appalachian Trail in Harpers Ferry National Park. I'd have passed right by it a week earlier, if I hadn't stumbled across Conor's body first.

It's not just one rock – it's several slabs of rock of various sizes, some of them piled on top of one another. The formation is partway up a ridge and allows a fine view of Harpers Ferry, the confluence of the Potomac and Shenandoah rivers, and the surrounding hills.

That view impressed Thomas Jefferson. He once stood there and proclaimed that the scenery was worth crossing an ocean for. I don't know if I'd cross an ocean for it, but it *is* pretty.

At some point in the 1800s, the National Park Service decided it would be a good idea to stabilize the top rocks with red sandstone pillars. So the formation isn't quite as impressive anymore as it would have been in Jefferson's day.

The Park Service doesn't exactly want people climbing around on the slabs, either. But rangers can't be everywhere, and I got the feeling Rufus had never met a rule he didn't immediately want to break. He clambered up onto the flat surface next to the braced slab and then helped Gail and me up.

I felt it as soon as I stood next to the balanced rock: The Otherworld, bleeding through. I've said Harpers Ferry was a liminal place, positioned as it was at the place where two powerful rivers meet. That aetherial power seemed to be focused here. "It's a gateway," I said.

"You bet it is." Gail paced the length of the rock, letting the fingers of one hand hover just above the surface. "It reminds me of a Neolithic passage tomb, except there aren't any dolmens on the sides for support – only the roof." She ducked her head to look under the rock, and shook her head. "Graffiti," she said with disgust. "People have to leave their mark everywhere, never mind whether they're defacing sacred space or not."

"So what's your plan?" I asked Rufus. "How do we call Collum?"

"Easy peasy. We walk around the rock there and call him."

I eyed him dubiously. "The Otherworld's a big place. You think he'll hear us?"

"Raney," he said with exaggerated patience. "That rock is going to act like a megaphone. If Collum is *anywhere* in the Otherworld – anywhere at all – he won't be able to avoid hearing it."

I flashed him a thumbs up. "Let's do it." He and I joined Gail next to the braced rock, and we began circling it, single file, and chanting, "Collum Barth, come to us! Collum Barth, come to us!"

We'd made a couple of circuits and were beginning the third when a voice called up from below, "All right, already! I heard you."

"Told you it would work," Rufus said, as I hopped down to give Collum a hug. "Jeez. Get a room, you two."

"Oh, leave them alone," Gail said. "They've been through a lot."

I pulled away from my favorite gnome. "We've all been through a lot. And it's only going to get worse from here."

"All right, Raney," said Gail. "You insisted we get together. What do you want us to do?"

"Me?" I squeaked. "I'm not in charge. I just thought we should compare notes. I know I've been changed, thanks to Cassius's ritual – my eyes are a different color and I'm faster on land, although not lots faster. I can't be the only one whose abilities morphed."

"Let's sit down," Gail suggested. We all took seats on the nearby retaining wall.

"We need to lay all our cards on the table," Collum said. "What are our strengths and weaknesses? What are we better at now that we've been through Cassius's crucible? And how can we use all of that to attack Drake and keep the wight locked away?"

"Do we *need* to keep the wight locked away?" Rufus asked.

Collum's mouth dropped open. "What are you, chaotic evil?"

Rufus laughed. "Sometimes. But right now I'm playing devil's advocate. Land wights are part of the natural order of things, right? I imagine they were put here for a specific purpose – to keep the Earth from being damaged by the other creatures who live on her. This one has been sequestered for so long that humans have had free rein to destroy the planet." He shrugged. "Maybe you should have never sequestered the wight in the first place."

"You have no idea why we did what we did," Collum said stubbornly. "You don't know what it was like when that thing was loose. Maybe in the long run, the Earth would have been saved from human destruction, but only because humanity itself would have been destroyed." His eyes narrowed. "When did salamanders become such authorities on land wights, anyway?"

"Dude, I'm just saying you should consider the possibility," Rufus said. Then his lips curled in a wicked smile. "Besides, a wight would be an amazing weapon to unleash on Drake and his scummy buddies."

"No," Collum said. "It's too dangerous. I wouldn't be able to control it."

"What if we all helped?" I asked. "Wasn't that the point of this joining or whatever happened to us? Aren't we supposed to be a team now?" I nudged him with my elbow. "What's *your* superpower, rock boy?"

He raised an eyebrow at me. Then he relented. "Okay, fine. I maintain the gates between this world and the Otherworld."

Collum is *the gate*. I snapped my mouth shut. Then I said, "How does that work, exactly?"

He shrugged. "A little of this, a little of that."

"Collum…" I glowered at him.

"I *pull* the materials I need to me," he said. "Remember when I made you the aquamarine? I knew which minerals I needed and I pulled them to me. It's instinct." He paused, head cocked. "Although it's been a little easier to do certain things since I woke up. I've never been able to wield Fire, Air, and Water the way I can now." He pointed nonchalantly at the rock at his feet; a spring bubbled up for a moment where none had been before. Then the rock itself seemed to catch fire, boiling the water away. A light breeze dispersed the steam, leaving nothing behind except a slight scorch mark on the rock. The whole thing took less than a minute.

He looked up at us. "My eyes changed color, too. They used to be brown."

"Mine were gray," said Rufus. "The color of ashes. Now there's brown and blue in them."

Gail sighed. "Mine were bright green. Did you know only two percent of people worldwide have green eyes? I loved having eyes that were such a rare color." She sighed again. "Now they're hazel, just like the rest of you. At least I can still fly."

"You can fly?" I asked, impressed.

She nodded. "I go where the wind takes me. Sometimes I hear or smell things on the wind. Sometimes it takes me where it needs for me to go." She paused. "It's been a little harder to get off the ground since this morning. But that's not necessarily a bad thing. I've been known to get carried away at inopportune moments." She smiled crookedly and ducked her head.

"Can you aim the wind?" Collum asked. "Or tell it to blow softly or spin up in a gale?"

She examined her nails. "I've been known to do that, yes."

"Don't be embarrassed," I said. Her head came up in surprise. "And don't be reticent about using your power when the time comes. You're here with us for a reason."

Her smile hardened. "You don't have to worry about me. I've never been reticent in my life."

I was suddenly glad she was on our side. "And you, Rufus?" I said, turning to him. "I mean, I know you can melt a phone with your bare hands."

He clucked his tongue. "That was a parlor trick. Plus that asshole had it coming." He grinned, then sobered. "I can call up Fire and direct it without it hurting me. My power seems more grounded now, and I can raise a bigger wind to fan the flames, too."

"And you get angry at the drop of a hat," I said. He didn't argue, so I turned to Collum. "And *you* can be stubborn."

"Me? No way," he said with a smirk.

"Yes way," I replied. "Gail is Airy to a fault. And I get weepy too easily."

"Sounds like a great team," Rufus said. "So what's our plan?"

"We should train together," said Collum. "That's what superheroes do in the movies."

Rufus stood and began pacing. "We don't have time for that. We need to get moving."

"What's the rush?" asked Gail.

Rufus glanced at me. "When I visited Farmington in the hospital, he told me Drake plans to blow the top off that mountain sometime over the next couple of days." He looked directly at Collum. "If we don't get moving, your wight will be released, whether you like it or not."

"Maybe it's a good thing, then," I mused, while the guys glared at one another.

"Maybe what's a good thing?" asked Gail.

"I keep running into this reporter from the local paper. This afternoon, I got tired of him poking around and following all the wrong

113

clues – so I told him about how Conor didn't drown and that Drake would do anything to get his latest project finished." I shook my head. "I'm not sure I made a dent. I've never met another reporter who's so thick that he wouldn't recognize a scandal if someone gave it to him gift-wrapped." I snorted. "But with any luck, Allen will hassle Drake enough to give us cover for whatever we decide to do."

"Which is?" Collum asked. "We still don't have a plan."

"Let's just go up there and confront the guy," Rufus said. "We can play it by ear."

"That sounds like the sort of approach that would get us all killed," I said. We glared at each other for a moment.

"How about this?" said Gail, breaking the tension. "Tonight, I'll do a flyover. Sort of get the lay of the land, make sure we know exactly where Drake is."

"A reconnaissance run," I said. "That sounds like a great idea."

"I think so, too," said Collum. "Once we have your report, Gail, we can meet again tomorrow and figure out how to attack him most effectively."

"Sounds perfect," I said. "Let's say lunch at the Private Ensign. Maybe one o'clock?"

Rufus threw up his hands. "Great. More planning. I mentioned that we have to *move*, right? The sooner, the better?"

"Yeah, I heard you," Collum said. You could tell when he was mad. He didn't turn red like Rufus did, but he'd get this portentous tone to his voice – like he was the Voice of the Earth and therefore outranked you, so you needed to *listen* to him. "I just don't think it will do us any good to go off half-cocked. We're only going to have one shot at the guy. It would be good for us to not blow it."

"Guys, guys," I said. "Where did Gail go?"

"Off to do reconnaissance," came her whisper on the wind. "I'll calllll yooooooou…"

114

"Sounds good," I said to the air. "Whoever hears from her first calls the others." I glanced at Collum. "Oh."

"Seriously," said Rufus. "Get a phone, dude."

"It's on my to-do list," Collum replied.

CHAPTER 13 – SUNDAY'S NOT OVER YET

I declined Rufus's offer of a ride home.

After he left, I turned to Collum, who was looking at me expectantly. Okay, avidly.

"So this may be a little awkward," I said, "but my mother's in town."

His face fell. "For how long? When did she get here?" And after a beat, "Can I meet her?"

"Wow," I said with a laugh. "Let me take these one at a time."

He laughed self-consciously. "Of course. Sorry."

"No worries," I said with a reassuring smile. Then I took a breath. "Okay. Mom arrived while we were…wherever we were. In the crucible thing. I guess Shenandoah got word to her that things were getting interesting here and she decided to just show up. I don't know how long she's staying."

"But she's staying with you."

"Yeah. I mean…" It suddenly occurred to me what day it was. "Oh, crap. It's Sunday. I was supposed to check out of that place today. Or else extend my stay."

"You never contacted the owner?"

"Things have been a little hectic," I said in my defense. "Hang on." I pulled out my phone and checked the Airbnb app. "Huh," I said, scrolling through the offerings for Harpers Ferry. "That's weird. The house isn't listed."

"The owner took it off Airbnb?" he asked. "But it was there when you booked it, right?"

"I didn't actually book it," I said with a grimace. "My good friend Cindy Hartley set it up for me."

"Who?"

"Officer Cindy Hartley," I said. "Harpers Ferry Police. The cops wanted to me to stick around town, but I hadn't planned on staying the night here and so I didn't have a reservation anywhere. So Cindy called her friend, who owns the place." I sank to a seat on top of the stone retaining wall. "I really don't want to have anything to do with the cops right now."

"I don't want *any* of us to get anywhere near the cops right now," he said in agreement. "Is there contact info for the owner in the apartment?"

"That's a good question. Usually, these places have a guest directory. Like a three-ring binder with the check-in and check-out times and all the rules and the cable channels and stuff." I thought for a moment, then shook my head. "I don't remember seeing one in this unit, though. I guess I'm gonna have to call her."

"Can I come with you?" he asked. "I mean, is it okay with you if…"

I shrugged. "I'm going to have to take care of this before anything else happens. So I guess you might as well."

We headed down the stairs to town. "What's your mother like?" he asked. "I don't think I've ever met an undine before."

I gave him a smirk over my shoulder. "You've met *me*."

"That's different. You're only half undine."

"I'm undine in all the ways that count," I said.

He was silent for a moment. "Sorry," he said at last.

"For what?"

"I didn't mean to insult you."

"You didn't insult me," I said, surprised. "I stated a fact. Everything an undine can do, I can do, too. The only difference is that I have a mortal soul." I threw a look back at him. "What's the difference between you and a full-on gnome?"

He huffed a laugh. "Well, for starters, I don't wear a pointy red hat."

I rolled my eyes. "Your gray beard is missing, too. Besides that."

"Besides that," he repeated. He was silent for a couple of steps. "Well. Most gnomes live in caves and a lot of them work as miners. And I don't do either of those things."

"You're the gate," I said.

He stopped short. "What did you say?"

I stopped, too. "That's what Tiger said in my dream." Then I whacked my forehead with the heel of one hand. "The cat! I haven't been to see Tiger today!" I quickened my pace. "I hope she's still speaking to me. We should stop there on the way. Except I don't have any food with me."

"Relax," Collum said, laughing. "She's been fed. That's where I was when you guys put out your A.P.B. for me."

It was my turn to stop and stare at him. "She let you in?"

He shrugged. "We're coming to an understanding."

"Uh-huh. I'll bet."

"We are, honest. She understands that when she's hungry and I show up with tuna, she'll get fed if she lets me in." He gave me a goofy grin. "Let's go and get your housing situation straightened out."

That turned out to be a very good idea. When we got to my street, a black sedan was parked at the curb in front of the place, some guy in a suit was standing in the yard with his back to me, and Mam was giving him a hard time at the top of her lungs.

"Uh-oh," I said, breaking into a run. Collum jogged after me.

"Raney!" Mam said in relief as I reached the sidewalk. "Would you please tell this person that I have a right to be here?"

The man in the suit turned and dazzled me with a thousand-watt smile. "You really are Raney Meadows," he said, and offered a well-manicured hand for me to shake. "It's such a pleasure to meet you. I'm Alex Drake."

Rufus was right. The guy was straight out of Central Casting. He was tall – more than a head taller than Collum – and lean, with dark hair perfectly coiffed to accentuate the gray at his temples. His eyes were the shade of blue that could only have come from tinted contacts. His dark gray suit was impeccably tailored, his white shirt was unwrinkled despite the August heat, and his tie sported little mallards on a field of navy blue. His shoes looked very expensive.

I tried not to stutter as I shook his hand. "Mr. Drake. Or should I call you Representative Drake?"

He waved his free hand. "Please. Call me Alex. I'm a big fan of your work." He beamed at me. "I saw the article in the *Sentinel* and I said to myself, 'What a coincidence that Cindy would call me for a favor for a witness, and it turns out the witness is my favorite actress? I'll just have to go on over and say hello.' But I couldn't get here until today. The people's business, you know. And then you weren't here, but this woman was." He nodded briefly at Mam, who was still seething. "And well, you can imagine how confused I was."

"He told me to get out!" Mam exploded.

"She's my mother," I said. "She just arrived today. Unexpectedly."

"Oh, well, in that case I'm terribly sorry," he said, nodding again at Mam without breaking stride. "But if there will be two people staying in the apartment, I'll have to charge more." He glanced dubiously at Collum. "And a third person is definitely not allowed."

"You own this place?" Collum said. "Raney was under the impression that it was an Airbnb."

"And you are…?" Drake inquired.

"Collum Barth," he said. "And there's no third person staying here. I live out in the county."

I guessed that was true, as far as it went. "Mr. Drake – Alex – I'm glad you're here, actually, because I need to extend my reservation and I couldn't find the place on Airbnb."

"Odd," he said, as if it weren't really odd at all. "Of course, I'd be happy to extend. Normally. But unfortunately, I have another guest coming in tonight. Which is another reason why I stopped by." His expression turned crafty. "To settle up."

"Oh, I see," I said faintly. "Well, let me go on in and pack. Like I said, I forgot I was going to need to be out today." I headed to the front door and dropped the wards, then turned the knob.

Behind me, Mam screamed and Collum yelled. Something banged into me from behind, knocking me flat across the threshold.

"I got it, boss!" a male voice yelled. I raised my head to see a brutish lout standing next to the coffee table, holding a thumb drive high in the air.

"Excellent," Drake said, stepping over me. He took the drive from the goon and pocketed it. He turned to me, sneering, as I got to my feet. "You thought you could outsmart me, didn't you? What a terrible actress you are, Ms. Meadows. I've known all along that you had this."

"That doesn't belong to you," Collum said, crowding in after me. "It was my brother's. Give it to me!"

"Not a chance," said Drake. He looked Collum up and down. "Your brother, hmm? What a despicable piece of work he was. He thought he could stop progress – but there's *no* stopping progress. This development will revitalize West Virginia's coal industry. The Mountain State will no longer be the laughingstock of America. We will be on top again – and *I'll* be the one to do it. The voters will love me for it. They'll elect me to Congress." He paused, a dreamy look on his face. "Why, I might even ride their regard all the way to the White House." He looked down his nose at Mam and me. "Get out."

"I need to pack," I said.

He pointed peremptorily at the door behind me. "Get. Out."

A breeze blew in through the open doorway, ruffling the curtains.

Collum, fists clenched, took two steps toward Drake and his henchman. The wind held him back. "Not that way," it whispered.

He and I traded a surprised look. *Gail?*

Collum turned his attention to Drake. "We can do this the easy way," he said, "or the hard way. You can give me the thumb drive and we'll let you leave here peacefully."

"Or?" Drake said gleefully. "You have no bargaining chips, little man. I own the house. I have the drive. You have nothing at all." He turned to his goon. "Get them out of here."

The breeze blew up into a vicious vortex. Lamps fell over and shattered. Curtains and window blinds whipped back and forth. Papers on the coffee table flew up and swirled around the room.

"What's happening, boss?" cried the goon, still on his backside.

"Stop that this minute!" Drake yelled at us.

"We're not doing anything!" I yelled back truthfully.

"Yet," Collum muttered. And he set his shoulders and planted his feet. "Hold on," he said to Mam and me.

We grabbed each other just as the floor began to shudder.

I didn't want to be left out of the fun, so I stretched my senses to the water in the kitchen pipes. In moments, a river coursed through the living room.

"You'll pay for the damage you're doing!" Drake yelled as the torrent swirled around his calves. His threat would have been more effective had the cataract not sent a free-floating dinette chair sailing into the backs of both knees, knocking him down. His perfectly tailored slacks were soaked. I imagined his shoes would never recover.

Collum strode confidently through the tumult, reached into Drake's breast pocket, and retrieved the drive. "Out," he said, gesturing toward the door.

I turned up the current as the breeze kicked up another notch. Our intruders floated out the door, which shut behind them with a satisfying click. Immediately, the shaking stopped. I slammed up the wards and looked above me. "Thanks, Gail."

"What are teammates for?" came the whispered reply.

The breeze gentled and warmed as I drained the water away through every crack and crevice I could find. Before long, everything was set to rights again.

Gail wafted away without materializing. Maybe she didn't want us to know how she did it just yet. Or more likely, she had gone outside to make sure Drake and his ugly buddy were good and gone. In any case, I hugged Mam and Collum, in that order.

"You can't stay here," he said.

I was already on my way to the bedroom. "I know. I'll be out in a minute – just need to throw my stuff in my backpack."

"Where will we go?" Mam said, following me into the bedroom.

I shrugged as I emptied dresser drawers. "We could stay at Conor's house, I guess. I'm sure Tiger wouldn't mind. She'd love having someone there to scratch her chin and clean out her box every day again."

Collum stopped at the doorway. "Or you could stay with me," he said.

I smiled at him. "Thanks, but one of us needs to have cell phone reception."

"Ouch."

"Seriously, we'll be fine at Conor's." I brushed past him to get to the bathroom, lingering a moment to put my hand on his chest.

He covered it with his own, and then raised my palm to his lips. I didn't blush when he did it. But then I noticed Mam watching us with a sappy smile on her face, and did.

A few minutes more and we were good to go. Collum ducked his head outside to make sure the coast was clear, then waved us on. I dismissed my wards for the last time, making sure everything in the house was as open and unguarded as I'd found it.

Collum insisted on carrying Mam's suitcase, for which I gave him mad props.

As we made our way across town in the twilight, he said, "Maybe you're right. Maybe it's better if you're not with me, since I have this." He patted a pocket where he'd stashed the thumb drive.

I winked. "You go ahead and keep it."

He blinked. Then he laughed aloud. "I wondered why you were so calm when Drake's boy grabbed it."

I grinned broadly. "Yep, he was very nearly the proud owner of Barney's Greatest Hits."

CHAPTER 14 – MONDAY AT LAST

Mam and I spent a relaxing morning settling in at Conor's place – as much as we could relax, knowing the whole thing could come to a head before sundown. Tiger cozied up to Mam, even though she knew Mam was an undine. *She's not going to liquefy while she's sitting next to me.*

"True enough," I said.

So it's fine. She gives good head scratches.

"I'm glad you approve," I said dryly.

The Private Ensign had not, in fact, exploded, nor had it suffered any damage at all from our time in the crucible. I wondered idly who had set Allen Owings on my tail that day. Probably Drake, I decided, via the local cops.

When I arrived at the restaurant, Cassius waved me off. "New meeting place," he said. "Gather at the Point."

"The point of what?" I asked.

He frowned. "The Point. The park that overlooks the confluence of the two great rivers."

"Oh," I said. "Sorry. Why?"

"This place may be compromised," he said.

His tone sent a chill down my spine. "Compromised? Like in a spy movie? That kind of compromised?"

He sat silently, as if that answered my question.

Suddenly I wanted someone in charge who knew what they were doing. "Are you coming to the meeting?"

He smiled, showing broad, even teeth. "No. My part in this is done."

Swell. Despite my misgivings, I thanked him for everything and headed downhill to the meeting place. Something told me the Private Ensign would have a different bouncer the next time I stopped by.

It was another hot, humid day. I maneuvered through the Lower Town, dodging slow-moving visitors in shorts who complained endlessly about the heat.

Rufus was already there, pacing. "Stop," I told him in greeting. "You're scaring the tourists." And in fact, a few folks enjoying the cool breeze off the water were eyeing him oddly and giving him a wide berth.

"Maybe they *should* be scared," he muttered. "Where's the leprechaun?"

"Would you quit calling him that?" I said.

"Right here," Collum said behind me. He hooked an arm around my shoulders and turned a gimlet eye toward the rivers. Below us, several kayakers in brightly-colored craft navigated the right turn from the mouth of the Shenandoah into the broader Potomac. I longed to be down there with them, but *in* the river, dissolving my cares away. Then I glanced at the set of Collum's features and realized the kayakers meant something very different to him, and felt ashamed that I'd even entertained the notion of abandoning this task, even for a minute. There would be time later for self-care. Right now, justice had to be served.

An errant breeze swirled around us, dancing. Then Gail appeared, as if she'd been standing with us all along. "That's a neat trick," I said.

"Thank you," she said modestly.

"Okay, Windy," said Rufus impatiently, "what do you know?"

Her laughter tinkled down the scale. "Are we all going to have code names? Marvelous! Collum is the Leprechaun, I'm Windy, and – what shall we call Raney?"

"The Torrent," I said with a burst of inspiration. "And Rufus is the Madman." I flashed him an overly-sweet smile. He glowered back.

"We still need a team name," she went on.

"I'm still voting for Elemental Thugs," I said.

124

"Can we get on with this?" Rufus said, raising his voice.

"Oh! Of course. Sorry," Gail said, although she looked as if she wasn't a bit sorry. "Well. After I left you all last evening, I tracked our target to the Airbnb where Raney – sorry, the Torrent – was staying."

Rufus's eyes widened. "What?"

She ignored him. "I arrived just as he and his henchman pulled up at the curb. I observed the subject make an attempt to get in the house, but Raney's wards repelled them. Then Raney's mother came around from the back of the house and an argument ensued."

"Which is when Collum and I arrived," I said.

"Right. When you dropped the wards, the henchman came rushing out of the car."

I nodded. "I assumed as much." I turned to Rufus. "Drake's goon grabbed the thumb drive from the coffee table and gave it to his boss. And then we got it back." I looked at Collum and Gail expectantly.

Gail picked up the thread of the narrative. "I spun up a little hurricane, Raney brought a river, and Collum shook the foundations. We literally brought the subject to his knees." She couldn't help smiling at that. "Then Collum got the thumb drive back and we sent the two of them packing."

Rufus put a hand to his forehead. "I can't decide whether this is a good thing or a bad thing," he muttered.

"How so?" Collum asked. "You're not saying we should have let him take the drive, are you?"

"Of course not. But we've tipped our hand. Now he knows what we're capable of."

"No, he doesn't," I said. "He's had a taste of our abilities, but he doesn't know the extent of them. Look, Drake doesn't have any magical ability – of that I'm certain. The way he's been bumbling around, trying to get past my wards, proves it. He used a *crowbar*, for goodness' sake, as if that would have any effect on a magical ward." I shook my head in wonder. The humans were all so *thick* here.

"That may have been that reporter, though," Collum said. "That's what you said at the time."

"I did, yeah. But the more I think about it, the more I think it was Drake the whole time."

"So who's behind Drake?" Collum asked. "Shenandoah told you an ancient evil had awakened. We know she didn't mean the wight. And if She didn't mean Drake, who's left?"

Gail cleared her throat. "If you'll let me finish my report," she said.

Rufus waved an arm toward her, palm up. "By all means."

"Thank you," she said, and cleared her throat again. "After I left Collum and Raney, I followed the subject back to his office, where another man was waiting for him. The first name of this other man is Damien. I didn't get his last name. But from what the two of them discussed, it seems this Damien is bankrolling this project, as well as the subject's political campaign."

"So he has lots of money," I said.

"Not only that," she said, "but even from a distance, I could feel the magic rolling off of him in waves."

The four of us exchanged glances. "How strong is he?"

"Strong," said Gail.

Everybody was silent for a moment, digesting this information. It looked like I was going to have to be the one to name the fear we all were feeling. "Too strong for us?" I asked her.

"I don't know."

Collum took in a deep breath and said, "Welp, I guess there's one way to find out." He looked at Gail. "Did these guys talk about their next move?"

"I was getting to that," she said with a touch of exasperation. "Honestly. And you all say *I'm* flighty. Anyway, yes, they said they planned to go up to Lost Falls first thing this morning and get ready for what they called the big blow."

126

"This *morning?*" Rufus cried. "You knew that, but you let us stand here and jabber this whole time?"

"They haven't done anything *yet,*" she said defensively. "I've just come from there. It takes time to set blasting caps and the like."

"But none of the rest of us can fly," Rufus said, as if it ought to have been glaringly obvious to her. "It will take us hours to drive up there."

"No, it won't," Collum said. "I know a shortcut."

"From here to Lost Falls," Rufus said.

"That's right."

Rufus eyed him dubiously. "Where is it? Because the only route I know goes up and around a couple of mountains."

"It's through the Otherworld," Collum said.

We all paused – but only for a second. Then Rufus said, "Let's go."

"What about lunch, though?" Gail asked. "I've been flying all morning and I'm hungry. Can we stop for something on the way?"

"Is fast food okay?" Collum asked. "And you – stop giving her a hard time," he said to Rufus as the Madman rolled his eyes. "The gate's not here anyway, and there's a place on the way."

"Fine," said Rufus. "But we're getting it *to go.*"

Comfortably full of burgers and fries, Collum led us out of town on the part of the A.T. I had missed hiking the week before. The air was still and close, the buzz of cicadas rising and falling irrhythmically. In seconds, I had sweated through my technical t-shirt.

About ten minutes down the trail, Collum slowed, looking for something. "This is it," he said to himself, and turned left, down a steep slope. Rufus crashed after him. Gail and I shrugged to each other and began picking our way down. I was so busy trying to find a route that didn't impact the native flora that I almost missed my stop – a stony ledge on the hillside where the guys were already waiting.

"Do you do your own stunts?" Rufus asked.

"Generally," I said. "Why?"

"No reason. You seemed kind of tentative coming down, is all."

I curled my lips up at one corner. "On set," I informed him, "I'm not trying to leave no trace."

He looked upslope, a guilty look on his face. "Oh," he said, as Gail joined us.

"Everybody good?" Collum said quietly. "Here we go. Stick close to me." And he turned to the wall behind us, took a step, and vanished.

"Is this like Platform 9 ¾?" Gail said in delight.

"Go," I said, poking Rufus, who was closest to the spot where Collum had disappeared.

I don't know what I'd thought it would be like – nausea, or a buzzing in my ears, or a sensation of falling. *Some*thing, anyway, to mark the transition from one world to the next. But there wasn't anything. One second I was walking head-on into a granite rock face, and the next I was on an overgrown path with the rock face behind me. The sky was the same blue, the undergrowth the same greens and grays, the path the same dusty brown. Collum and Rufus waited just a few steps ahead.

"Oh my!" Gail said as she stepped out behind me. "That wasn't what I expected at all."

"Come on," said Collum, heading off down the trail. "We've got about a twenty-minute walk ahead of us. This path isn't built for speed."

I scooted ahead of Rufus to talk to Collum. "It looks like it was well-used at one point. Doesn't anyone maintain it?"

"Not anymore."

There was such sorrow in his voice that I laid a hand on his arm. "You're the last of a breed, aren't you? Like the wight."

"Not exactly. But there used to be a lot more of us." He whacked a low-hanging vine aside. "A *lot* more of us."

"What happened?" I asked. But he didn't answer.

"Magic's dying out everywhere," Rufus said from behind me. "There used to be a lot more salamanders, too."

"Is that why we're all half-human?" Gail asked. "Elementals mating with humans to keep the race alive?"

"Not me," I said. "Mam mated with my father to give me a soul."

"Trading existence for immortality," Rufus mused. "I'm not sure that's such a great bargain."

I shrugged. "Nothing I can do about it. The deed is done."

"Have you ever met your father, Raney?" Gail asked.

"No. I've seen photos, but that's all. Mam and he split when I was very young. She's been in hiding from him ever since."

"I wonder why," Gail mused.

I didn't have an answer for her. To be honest, I'd never thought to ask Mam why we'd kept moving. It was simply a fact of life, like my ability to become one with water.

Presently, our path began to follow the bank of a stream. Soon I could hear the rush of water, a sound that always gladdened my heart. But this time I heard something else, too: a rhythmic pounding, like a chisel on rock.

"This way," Collum said. He stepped off the trail into a thicket and disappeared. This time, we were ready – we plunged in after him.

We came out at the edge of a clearing. Next to us were a pile of crates prominently marked, "Danger – Dynamite – Highly Flammable" and coils of fuse material on giant reels that were at least three feet in diameter. Across from us, technicians swarmed the rock face around the most beautiful waterfall I'd ever seen. And between us and them, supervising the workers, stood two men.

"There he is," Gail breathed. "Can you feel it? The *evil* rolling off that guy?"

One of the men was Drake. The other one I didn't recognize until he turned slightly, allowing me to see his profile.

"Oh, no," I said.

"What is it?" Collum asked, clutching my arm. "You're white as a sheet."

"That's my father," I said.

CHAPTER 15 – THE WORST MONDAY OF MY LIFE

In an instant, associations and implications tumbled into place in my head. I'd known Mam had hidden us from my father because he could hurt us, but it had never occurred to me to ask why.

When I was a child, Mam had read to me from a book of Irish fairy tales. One of my favorites was the one about the selkie – a magical seal who could shed her skin and become human. One day, a man stole the selkie's skin while she was in human form, and refused to give it back to her unless she became his wife. The poor thing agreed – and yet he kept the skin hidden from her. She kept his house and bore him children, and still he kept her skin locked away in a chest.

There came a day when he was careless and left the key in the lock. She waited until he left for work, and then she unlocked the chest and reclaimed her skin. She told her children not to be sad for her, because she was going back where she belonged. Whereupon she donned her skin and dove into the sea, and they never saw her again.

The situation the selkie wife found herself in was not exactly like my mother's, but it was close enough for little me to equate the two. They were both creatures of the sea, for one thing. For another, the selkie's husband would likely do her harm if he found her again – and as I grew older, I realized he had done her harm from the first, by stifling who she was in order to make her into who he needed her to be. In any case, the selkie had a profound motive for escaping from him and making sure he could never hurt her again. And I was luckier than the selkie's children. My mother had kept me. Theirs had left them behind.

I never thought about who my father may have been. Perhaps Mam had glamored me to keep me from asking questions. Now, though, seeing him in the flesh for the first time, I began to understand why she might have done it – because evil *did* roll off him in waves, just as Gail had said.

And another thought occurred to me: Maybe she hadn't chosen him as a mate to give me a soul. Maybe she hadn't had a choice in the matter.

And if my soul came from a man so inherently evil, what did that make me?

"Did you just say Damien Jones is your father?" said a voice at my elbow. I turned, still in shock, to find Allen Owings looking at me with interest.

"Who the hell are you?" demanded Rufus.

"Allen Owings, *Harpers Ferry Sentinel*," he said, flashing a card that said PRESS PASS at the top. "What are you all doing here?"

"More to the point, what are *you* doing here?" Rufus asked.

Allen pointed at me. "She told me to come."

I found my voice at last. "I did not!"

"Keep it down," Collum said, glancing at Drake and my father. He herded us all into the woods behind us.

I lowered my voice to a hiss. "I said you should investigate Drake. I didn't say you should follow us."

"But I didn't," he protested. "I've been here since sunup. I saw y'all come out from the woods and came over to talk to you." He puffed out his chest. "They're gonna blow the top off this mountain, you know."

"Yeah, and we're here to stop them," Collum said. "If that mountain blows, the repercussions will be tremendous. Harpers Ferry will probably cease to exist – and that's just for starters. The damage would extend all the way to Washington, D.C."

"You sure seem to know a lot about this, sir," Allen said eagerly. "Can I quote you? Are you a geologist?"

"My brother was a geologist," Collum said darkly. "Now he's dead."

"Our missing kayaker," I told Allen.

He took a step back. "Oh, my God. Really? This is… This is *huge*."

"Yeah," I said. "Yeah, it is."

Rufus stuck out a hand to Allen. "Rufus MacKay. I'm an organizer for Laborers' Union International. What do you know about Damien Jones? I've heard his name a few times, but nobody seems to know much about him."

"He's the money man," Allen said promptly. "He founded Atlantic-Omaha Corporation. Anything you use that's made from wood pulp, his company probably made it. Paper towels, toilet tissue, you name it."

"Seems fitting somehow," Gail said.

Allen went on, "He's taken some of his millions and founded a shadow PAC that bankrolls candidates who will do the bidding of corporate America. Of all the people encouraging Drake to run for Congress, he's been the most vocal. Drake's been teetering on the brink of bankruptcy for the last several years. I've heard he agreed to run for Congress only if Jones lent him the money for this project." He nodded toward the waterfall.

"No way," Rufus said. "Drake isn't that smart."

"He's sneaky, though," Collum said. "And ambitious. He wants more than a seat in Congress."

"You're kidding," Allen said, and laughed. "Who'd vote for a failed know-nothing businessman for President?"

As they talked, I found myself pulled away, toward the clearing again. "I've got an idea," I said. "Maybe this doesn't have to end in violence." And I started toward where my father stood with Drake.

"Raney! Raney, stop!" Collum called. But it was too late. Whatever was impelling me on – whether it was a primal urge within me to meet my father or something more nefarious – it had a hold on me that nothing could shake.

The two men were concentrating so hard on the scene before them that neither one of them heard me approach. I waited until I was just a few feet away. Then I said, "Father?"

As one, they turned.

Drake spoke first. With a sneer, he said, "Well, well, well. If it isn't our little local celebrity. Run back to Hollywood, Ms. Meadows. There's nothing you and your friends can do to stop me now."

I heard him, but I had no voice to respond – for my whole attention was caught by the man standing next to him. The man with the chin and forehead just like mine. The man with molten red eyes. "Daughter mine," he intoned. His voice held bubbling depths where all moisture had long since steamed away. "How good it is to meet you at last. Long have I searched for you. Come to me." He held out both hands toward me. "Your mother should never have taken you from me."

I was all set to go to him – but his mention of Mam stopped me. "She had reasons for what she did," I said.

"None that made sense," he said. "Ondine was ever a bundle of emotions – nothing more." He shook his hands gently. "Come. Let me touch you, my sweet, the best and brightest fruit of my loins. Come, and let your father hold you."

My feet began moving of their own accord. I was drawn closer to those pulsing red eyes… closer… closer…

"Hey, Drake!" Rufus yelled behind me. "Catch!" A lit stick of dynamite sailed over my head toward the men.

"No!" I cried. I couldn't let my father die – not when I'd just met him. I pulled a stream of water from the falls, intending to put out the fuse. But distracted as I was, I misjudged the gap. Instead of dousing the flame, it hit the stick full on, knocking it well away from its intended target but soaking it in the process. Crystals began to form on the outside of the tube as it fell.

"Shit," Rufus said behind me. "This is gonna hurt." He dashed past me and fell prone on top of the explosive.

The technicians on the hillside must have been watching. "Fire in the hole!" one of them yelled, and they all scrambled for cover.

Behind me, Collum screamed, "Get back! Raney, get back!" But all I could do was stand there, transfixed, staring at Drake and the spot next to him where my father had been.

And then the dynamite blew.

I fell to the ground, ears ringing, as a massive fireball rose from the spot where Rufus had lain — where smoke now rose from a crater perhaps thirty feet across. I expected to be showered with little bits of Rufus — but no, a minute later our Madman pulled himself up on the edge of the hole and staggered toward me. His eyebrows had been burned off and his shirt and jeans were stained with powder burns, but the salamander had survived the fire.

"Shit," he said again, looking at the ruin of his clothing. "This was my favorite shirt, too."

Collum, Gail, and Allen ran toward us. "Are you all right?" Collum asked us both. His voice sounded muffled. Everything sounded muffled.

"I'll survive," Rufus said. "Don't ever do that again, okay, Raney?"

"Yeah, okay," I said, struggling to my feet. My hearing was clearing rapidly. "I don't know what got into me."

"Damien," Gail said. We all turned to look at her. "Damien got into you. I saw the currents of magic pulling you to him, but I didn't know what they were until you went after him." She shook her head and looked away. "What an idiot I am. I should have been more proactive."

"It's okay," I said, wrapping an arm around her. "You couldn't have known. None of us could have known." Then I burst into tears. "But I may never have a chance to meet my father again!"

"Oh, trust me," Rufus said. "You'll have another chance. He knows who you are now."

I stared at him, my tears drying up as fast as they'd begun. He was right. Not only did Damien Jones knew who I was — he knew what I did for a living. He knew where to find me. And he knew I had inherited my mother's Elemental ability.

For the Big Evil Guy, I would be quite the prize.

"Guys," Collum said, his voice strained. "We have another thing to worry about."

"Drake got away, didn't he?" Rufus looked around angrily. "We need to find him again. Gail, can you...?"

"Forget Drake," Collum said. "That hole you tore into the ground?"

"Yeah, what about it?"

Collum nodded toward it. "It goes to the Otherworld. And thanks to you capping it the way you did, the dynamite did more damage there than it did here."

"What are you saying?" Rufus said. "Spit it out, dude."

"The gate's gone," Collum said. "The wight is loose."

"What's a wight?" Allen asked.

"Stick around," said Rufus. "You're about to find out."

A roar issued from the gaping hole, and a mound rose from within it. It looked the way I'd imagined a cinder cone rising from a volcano's crater would look, except this mound was made of dirt, and it appeared to have been torn loose from the landscape. Scraggly roots dangled from its edges, and between the roots, I could see a face. Eyes black as coal glared out at us from under the mound of dirt.

One of the thicker roots raised of its own accord and pointed toward us. "You!" the wight said, its blackened mouth opening wide. "Gnome! You will pay for this!"

"You know this thing?" Rufus asked Collum in astonishment.

"We're acquainted," Collum said.

"Just how old *are* you?" I blurted.

"Never mind that, leprechaun," Rufus snapped. "Get over there and talk it down!"

"It doesn't work that way," Collum said, but he ambled toward the creature anyway.

Gail and I exchanged nervous looks. "What should we do?" I asked Rufus.

136

He glanced at us. "No idea," he confessed, and turned back to watch the show.

CHAPTER 16 – THE NEVER-ENDING MONDAY

The wight roared and vaulted out of the hole. I'd thought before that its head looked like a mound of dirt, but that wasn't even close. Now that we could see the whole creature, the mound was clearly a mountain. It was so big that partway up the slope, the treeline gave way to alpine tundra. I even caught the sparkle of snow in the shadows.

Its body was a sort of taproot, or maybe a joining of all the taproots of all the trees on its head. Its arms and legs were gangly branches of root systems.

I heard someone mewing like a kitten. It took a minute to register that it was me.

The wight roared again and began walking forward on its root-feet.

Allen squeaked. Then he fumbled with his camera and began snapping photos as if his life depended on it.

Collum had closed about half of the distance between the monster and us. Then he planted himself as if he, too, were a mountain. A smallish mountain, comparatively, but still. "Cloch!" he called. He pronounced the last two letters as if he were Tiger hacking up a hairball. "How goes it down there?"

The creature stopped. "Well enough," it rumbled.

"The food is good?"

Slowly, the wight nodded its massive head. "Yes, I suppose."

"And how's the wife?"

"Tolerable," it – or he, I guess – said.

Collum laughed. "Tolerable, he says. Women, eh?"

A deep throbbing sound emanated from the wight. The ground trembled. Clods of dirt showered down around him. "Aye, women," it rumbled.

Rufus snickered. Then he glanced at Gail and me, cleared his throat, and focused his attention on Collum and the wight again.

"Listen, Cloch," Collum said. "I hate to ask you to do this, but I need for you to get back in the hole and go back to the Otherworld."

Cloch's ebony gaze narrowed. "Why?"

"Because there is a man here in this world who wants to harm you. He wants the coal you've been guarding."

"He can't have it."

"That's right. That's why we set you to guard it."

"But only for a year and a day," the wight said. "Your father said after a year and a day, the danger would be past." His head tilted. "How long has it been, gnome? Has it been more than a year and a day?"

"Somewhat longer," Collum hedged.

"How long?"

"A lot longer," he admitted.

"How. Long?" the wight roared.

"Uh. A couple of centuries. Give or take."

The wight considered the information. "That long?" he said at last. His root-shoulders shrugged, releasing another shower of dirt. "The food's good."

Collum smiled in relief. "I'm glad. So you're not angry?"

"Oh, I'm angry, all right," said the wight. "Where is your father? I need to talk with him."

"He's not here."

"Well, get him."

Now Collum looked nervous. "It's not a thing that can be done in a minute," he said. "You see, my parents are in Ireland."

"Where's Ireland?" the wight asked.

"It's an island across the sea," Collum said. "A long, long way from here." Then he brightened. "But I know a shortcut. You could come with me."

The wight eyed him suspiciously. "Where's this shortcut, then?"

"Well, first we go back down the hole…"

"I knew it!" Cloch roared. "You are as faithless as your father before you, and his father before him! I've fulfilled my part of the bargain! I am not going back in that hole!" And he picked up a crate of dynamite and threw it at Collum.

A strong wind blew up and caught the box in midair, then gently lowered it to the ground.

"No more explosions," Collum said sternly. "And no arguments, Cloch. It's not safe up here for you. Back in the hole you go."

In a rage, Cloch began to jump up and down. Five, six, seven – by his eighth or ninth jump, my teeth felt like they would rattle out of my head. I could feel the tectonic plates below us grinding against one another and beginning to shift. When that shift happened, a new fault line would be created. The earth would literally move.

Collum looked over his shoulder at me. I could feel him doing his best to stabilize the movement, but he couldn't hold it forever. The plates needed some kind of cushioning. Some kind of…

It wasn't water, but it would work.

Deep below us, I found a pool of tar sands – oil mixed with sand, clay, and a little water – and began luring it toward the destabilizing rock. I figured the mixture would sort of grease the plates as well as providing a cushioning layer.

Cloch kept jumping. Collum gritted his teeth and held on. Rufus howled something and ran off toward the waterfall. Gail was nowhere to be seen.

At last, my nasty tar sands found their way to the trembling plates and began to flow around and between them. The plates were still vibrating, but the grinding had stopped. Thanks to the fluid around them, they couldn't move anymore.

Cloch screamed. He stopped jumping and balled up his root-fists. It was clear he planned another attack, but I couldn't figure out what it was.

Then I noticed the snow in the shadows on his head were melting. He was making his head into a volcano, and it was getting ready to blow.

"Rufus!" I yelled. "You're up!"

"Again?" he cried. He yelled to the remaining technicians on the hillside; they understood and fled. Then he took a running leap and landed on the side of Cloch's mountainous head.

Cloch reached up and began brushing madly at the side of his head. "Get off me, mortal!" he yelled.

But Rufus was good at dodging, and before long, he was near the peak. There, he stopped in dismay. "It's too big," he called to us. "I can't stop it from blowing!"

Cloch made that rumbling noise again, and this time it sounded evil. Then he held his nose and blew.

Puffs of smoke rose from the crest of his head.

My mind raced. *Think, Raney. Think! What puts out fire?*

Oh, duh.

"Get down!" I yelled to Rufus. "I've got this!" And as he leaped clear of the wight, I called on the river goddesses. *Mighty Potomac! Beautiful, deep Shenandoah! Help us subdue this wight, and I will be that much closer to avenging the fouling of your waters with the dead man's blood!*

"This wight is known to us," Shenandoah rippled in my head. "We will help you."

And as the volcano began to spew its fire, the rivers forced themselves to reverse their flow and push together up the Shenandoah's course, up into the mountains above the waterfall. The falls turned into a cataract, overspilling the pool at its base and drenching the wight with its spray.

Collum raised his arms in complicated patterns, directing the Earth to create dykes that would route the waters back to the rivers without flooding anything below.

Cloch was apoplectic. Three times he had attacked the gnome who wanted to sequester him again, and three times his actions had been thwarted. He readied himself for a third attack, but I couldn't think what it might be. Dynamite was created from natural substances. Earthquakes were natural phenomena. So were volcanoes. What else could he do?

I never found out. Before the river goddesses departed, they spoke to the wight. "Cloch," they called from the channel Collum had created for them. I could see their faces floating just under the water's rushing surface. "Our old and dear friend. We have missed you so."

The wight stopped. "Potomac? Shenandoah? Is it truly you?"

"We are here. The undine called us to your side."

I blinked. That wasn't how I would have put it, but okay. I was willing to play along.

"Undine?" The wight peered around the clearing. I sighed inwardly. Then I stepped out from the sheltering trees and gave Cloch a little wave.

The wight turned back to the goddesses. "This undine is known to you?"

"Yes," they said. "We have charged her with a task. A mortal man was killed untimely and his body was dropped into our waters. His blood has befouled us. The undine seeks the killer."

"He was no mortal," Collum said. "He was a gnome. My brother."

Cloch straightened once again to his full height. "An Earth Elemental!" His eyes narrowed. "This is what comes of sequestering wights! This is what comes of interfering with Nature!"

"You're right," Collum said, head bowed. "You're absolutely right. I had misgivings about my father's crazy plan from the start. But I couldn't talk him out of it, no matter how hard I tried. And our argument tore our family apart. Eventually my brother left. Then my parents left, and the other gnomes…" He paused, his lower lip trembling. "I am the last. When I am gone, the gate will be unguarded and the Earth will be undone."

"It will not," the wight rumbled. Collum's head snapped up. "Little gnome," Cloch went on, "you forget that I knew your father. He was a fine gnome, but stubborn. You could no more have persuaded him to drop his plan than I could swim in the ocean." He took a step toward Collum. "You and I have both suffered from his obstinacy. Let us together find another way — a better way — for all of us."

"Hear! Hear!" Gail cried.

"But how can we?" Collum said. His voice resonated with so much despair that my eyes welled with tears. "You *have* to go back in the hole, Cloch! It's not safe for you here!"

"Little gnome," said the wight, "it has always been safe for me here. I *am* this land."

I could feel the emotions warring in Collum's soul: on one hand, his fealty to his father and his desperation to make things right, and on the other, hope that there was a way out. For the wight. For his family. And most especially, for him.

Rufus said, "That's what I tried to tell you before, Collum. The wight endangered the mortals, not the other way around. They wanted Cloch tamed so *they* would be safe. And in making it safe for mortals, the land itself has been put in peril."

"You're talking gibberish!" Alex Drake strode forth from his hiding place, behind a convenient boulder out of the way of the cataract. "Humanity has been granted a Manifest Destiny by the grace of God! This land, and everything in it, was put here for *our* use!"

"But not for your exploitation," Rufus said. "And not for you to exploit other humans while you rape the land."

Drake turned purple. "Union scum. You people have been a thorn in my side ever since my family started this company!" he said. "Well, I'm tired of people like you and that geologist getting in my way!"

Cloch squinted one eye and looked at Collum. "Is this pipsqueak the mortal who killed your brother?"

"That's him," I said promptly. "His name is Alex Drake. And not only did he kill Conor, but he also plans to blow the top off this mountain to get to the coal seam you've been protecting for so long."

"Is that so?" He stretched out a long root and snatched up Drake by his collar.

"Put me down!" Drake hollered, his feet dangling a yard above the ground.

"What shall we do with him?" Cloch asked of Collum.

"No killing," said Collum.

"Agreed," said the wight. "It is not yet his time." He looked at me. "Undine?"

My mind went blank. All I could think of was *an eye for an eye*, and killing Drake was already off the table. "Why don't you let the rivers decide?" I said at last.

"So be it," said the wight, and dropped Drake into the channel.

He splashed mightily when he hit. "Get me out of here! I can't swim!" he cried. But the goddesses wrapped him in their graceful fronds, and eventually he was still.

His lack of movement alarmed me. "He's not dead, is he?" I blurted.

"No," said Potomac. "The gnome has decreed that he should not die. We will abide by his wishes."

"Do not worry. We shall take good care of him," Shenandoah said. "Undine, you have served us well. Our thanks to you."

"You're welcome," I said. "Any time."

"Please give your mother our regards," they said, and flowed away, taking Drake with them.

"I will," I whispered, certain they could hear me. Then I started. "My father!" I looked around wildly. "You guys, where did my father go?"

Rufus walked over to me. "All I know is he disappeared as soon as I threw the stick of dynamite at him." He put a hand on my shoulder. "I'm sorry. I couldn't figure out any other way to break his hold on you."

Tears spilled down my cheeks. "It's all right," I said, even though it wasn't.

Gail put a hand on Rufus's shoulder. "You did the right thing," she said. "Damien was not going to let her get away."

"He wants my mother," I said.

"No, he wants *you*," Gail said. "I know that much for sure."

I stared at her through my tears. "You mean all these years when he's been tracking us down, he hasn't been trying to get Mam back?"

"Well, I can't speak to that," she said. "I only know what the wind told me today. And today, it was you he wanted."

Maybe Mam hadn't been protecting herself all those years. Maybe she'd been protecting me.

"Don't worry," Gail said, patting my other shoulder. "I'm dead certain we haven't seen the last of Damien Jones."

"Don't sound so excited," I said.

"He may be your father, Raney, but he's bad news," said Rufus. "None of us should be looking forward to seeing him again. Least of all you."

I shrugged helplessly. "He's my father."

Collum approached, the wight trailing after him. He gave Rufus a crooked smile and said, "I'll work with her on that."

"What about you, me boyo?" said Rufus, stepping to one side to make room for Collum in our ring. "How are we gonna get you released from this hunk of rock?"

"It is done," Cloch said. "I have always been the guardian here. Now that I am back, I will resume my duties. And *you*, little gnome, may resume the life you had before your father saddled you with this one."

"Thank you, Cloch," said Collum. I wouldn't say he was overcome with gratitude – he was too stoic for that – but his face shone.

"No thanks needed. Two wrongs have been righted today. Not a bad day's work, eh?" He looked around and sighed gustily. "It is good to be home."

"I guess you need to go back to the Otherworld and fetch your wife," Rufus said with a merry grin.

Cloch gave him the old side-eye. "Her return may be delayed."

CHAPTER 17 – TUESDAY AT LAST

We had lost track of Allen Owings. The last thing I remembered was the sound of his shutter going lickety-split when Cloch clambered out of the hole.

I learned early Tuesday morning where he'd gotten off to.

"Have you seen the paper yet?" Rufus asked when Mam and I met him at the diner. He gave it a shove so hard that it nearly flew off the table. "Sorry. Don't know my own strength 'til I've had coffee."

"It's the other way around for normal people," I said. "Have you met Mam?"

"Not yet. But I've heard a lot about you," he said, half getting up to greet her. She smiled graciously and briefly took his extended hand. The waitress brought us glasses of water and dropped off menus as we took our seats.

Finally, I had an opportunity to glance at the front page. "Oh, jeez," I said in dismay. There we were – all four of us – surrounding Cloch, who was ready to blow his top.

Mam glanced at it. "At least he got your good side," she said, spreading her napkin in her lap. "Did he spell your name right?"

"You sound like Sid," I said. "My agent," I explained to Rufus. "Who I haven't heard from in a couple of weeks, come to think of it. What day is it? Tuesday? I wonder where I'm supposed to be today?"

"Duncannon, I think," Mam said. "What do you recommend, Rufus?"

"Don't let him order for you," I told her. "You'll end up with enough food for a week." My phone buzzed in my pocket. I extracted it and looked at the screen. "Speak of the devil," I said. "Would you please order scrambled eggs and bacon for me? Thanks." I slid out of the booth and answered the phone while walking to the parking lot. Fog hung in the valley like cotton candy, but the sun was up and the temperature was rising. I knew it would be gone soon.

"Sid, hey," I said. "I was just saying to Mam…"

"What the hell were you thinking?" he began.

I blinked. "When, specifically?"

"You're supposed to be lost in the wilderness!" he said. "Not spread all over social media with some cosplay troupe!"

"Cosplay? What are you talking about?"

"There are photos. Of you. And some giant mountainous *thing.*"

Uh-oh. "Calm down, Sid. Where did you see them?" I knew he didn't have a subscription to the *Harpers Ferry Sentinel.*

"On Instagram!"

And by extension, Twitter and Facebook and wherever else. Every media outlet in the country must have them by now.

I scanned the parking lot. Sure enough, a couple of cars had telephoto lenses sticking out of their windows. Their numbers, I knew, would multiply very shortly. This was exactly why I'd left Hollywood – eyes everywhere, following my every move.

The paparazzi were bad enough on a regular day. Things got worse when the gossip rags started paying them extra for signs that I was suffering from a bad breakup. If word got out that I was an undine, I would literally never have any peace.

I could hardly fault Allen Owings – the guy knew he had career gold and decided not to wait for the wire services to pick it up. But he had sure complicated my life.

I smiled and waved for the cameras. "Sid, I need to go."

"God damn it, Raney!"

"I'll call you back, I promise!" I ended the call, and with another cheery wave, I went back into the restaurant.

The food hadn't arrived yet. Mam and Rufus were making small talk with polite smiles all around, but they broke it off when I returned. I downed my glass of water and signaled the waitress for a refill.

148

"That bad, huh?" Mam asked, passing me her glass.

I downed it. "Worse. The photos are all over social media." I looked inquiringly at Rufus, who made a *by all means* gesture toward his own glass. I drank that, too, and sat back, my tummy sloshing.

"What does that mean, exactly?" he asked.

"It means Harpers Ferry is about to be overrun with paparazzi," I said. "It's going to get ugly here. I'm really sorry." My mind raced. "I need to get back on the trail. I should leave today."

"Don't be ridiculous," Mam said. "They'll follow you. They'll ambush you at the next town you come to. Maybe one of them will fall down a mountain while tailing you."

"And how would that be my fault?" I said. But I knew she was right – running away was risky now, and not just for me. I closed my eyes in resignation. "So what do I do?"

"Eat," Rufus said. "After that, we'll think of something."

The food arrived just then, which made the decision easy.

"So what's on tap for you today?" Mam asked Rufus as he attacked his double stack of pancakes.

"Going back out to the Hornbill work site," he said. "It's Farmington's first day back on the job."

I paused in mid-chew. "Didn't he have a shattered pelvis or something? I thought he was going to be out for weeks."

Rufus shrugged. "He's had some kind of miraculous recovery."

"How?"

"Magic, I guess," Rufus said, forking pancakes into his mouth. "Anyway, I want to make sure management doesn't hassle him into getting hurt again." He chewed and swallowed. "I'd also like to find out what they know about Drake's disappearance. It wasn't in the paper." He pointed toward the article with his fork, then speared a piece of sausage.

"Allen must have left before we resolved everything," I said. I flipped to the inside page where the rest of the photos were and glanced over them. Sure enough, they were all from the buildup to the battle. He must have scooted as soon as Cloch started toward us. And why not? Any sane person would have done the same thing. *I* would have done the same thing, if I hadn't just been in thrall to my father.

My father. Had he…?

Oh, yeah. He had.

I closed the paper, but not fast enough. Mam inhaled sharply. I cringed and turned to her, expecting a tongue lashing. I did not expect her expression of horror – or the sigh of resignation that rapidly followed it.

"Excuse me," she muttered, throwing aside her napkin and walking rapidly toward the door. I called the waitress over and asked for more water. "Maybe bring us a pitcher," I said. "Or two."

"You didn't tell her?" Rufus asked, nodding toward the front door. Mam stood just inside the vestibule with her back to us.

"I didn't know how," I said. I took a bite of egg, swallowed, and pushed my plate away. My appetite had fled.

Rufus went on demolishing his breakfast. I debated whether to go after Mam, but decided against it. Better to have this out at Conor's old place, behind Tiger's wards and mine – not in full view of whichever enterprising paparazzo had a long enough lens. "I should have talked to her last night," I said quietly.

"Probably." Rufus took a swig of coffee. "But you didn't, so here's where we are right now. Are you gonna eat your bacon?"

In response, I pushed my plate toward him.

"Thanks," he said, scooping my food onto his plate. "So what's the Leprechaun up to today?"

"I have no idea."

"He should be relieved of guard duty, right? Now that the wight is back?"

"I guess."

"But he still hasn't gotten a phone." He pointed his fork at me. "You should make sure he gets on that."

"I'll put it on my list," I said, managing a smile.

150

Mam resumed her seat. She drank a glass of water and then sat with her head down.

"Mam…" I started. But she waved me off. That made me feel worse than ever.

Rufus put down his fork at last. "Look. Let me drive you two back to Conor's old place. You can hardly walk there with a trail of cameras behind you."

Mam raised her head and smiled politely. "Thank you, Rufus. You are a good friend." Her smile turned sad. "My daughter has made good friends here."

"Good friends who will protect her," he said. "Although she's pretty good at protecting herself when she needs to." He looked at me as he said it. "Don't forget that, Raney."

Mam wrapped her toast in a paper napkin and I paid the bill. Rufus left the tip.

He stopped us in the vestibule. "Hang on a sec," he said, squinting at the sun. It got very bright around us. "Okay, let's go."

The brightness surrounded us as we went out to the car. "Did you put us inside a sun dog?" I said with delight.

He shrugged. "The sun's basically a ball of Fire, right?" Then he grinned. "Let's see those photographers get a clear shot of us through *this*."

"You need to teach me how to do it," I said as we reached the car. I let Mam take shotgun and climbed in back.

"You probably could," he said. "The trick is to find ice crystals in the air and play the sunlight off of them."

"Thanks for the tip. I'll work on it."

When we reached Conor's, I made sure the paparazzi would continue to be stymied by adding a bit of refraction to the wards surrounding the house. It didn't make the place disappear, but it pretty much guaranteed that any shot they got of us would be too blurry to use. I'd used the same trick for years in L.A., especially after the ex moved in.

Tiger met us at the door. *What did you bring me?* she asked, purring violently.

"Sorry," I said. "Rufus ate it all."

Salamanders, she huffed, and went off to lay in the sun.

I watched her go, delaying the inevitable. Finally I turned to my mother. "I'm so sorry," I began.

"You have nothing to be sorry for," she said. She sat on the living room sofa and clutched a throw pillow around her middle.

"Want some water?" I asked.

"No, I'm fine," she said automatically.

I filled a glass anyway and brought it to her. She downed it immediately. I refilled it and got another for myself. Then we sat in silence for a minute, not looking at one another – her on the sofa and me on the loveseat.

Finally I said, "I should have told you…"

At the same time, Mam said, "This is all my fault."

I stopped. "How is it your fault? I should have told you last night, but I couldn't."

"There wouldn't have been anything to tell if I hadn't gotten into this fix in the first place!" Her fingers knotted in the pillow as if she might tear it apart.

"Which fix?" I said. I tried to read her emotions, but they were so tangled I had trouble following any of the threads. I sent her a wave of love and reassurance as I said, "Maybe you should start at the beginning."

She looked directly at me. "You were not a mistake."

That made me sit up straighter. "I never thought I was."

"But you might, when I tell you…" She sighed. "I should never have gotten involved with him."

"Tell me," I said.

She took a deep breath and began.

~ ~ ~

152

Damien Jones was the most charismatic man I'd ever met. I was hundreds of years old by then – not a callow maiden at all – but there was something about him I could not… could not…

I could not escape him. Nor did I want to try.

Damien was wealthy then, and ruthless, but nothing like he is today. He always wanted to be the richest man in the world, but *rich* to him never meant just money. He wanted to have everything. Everything that was worth having. Anything anyone else coveted, he needed to have for himself.

The first time I saw him, he was standing naked on the veranda of his oceanfront estate. It was early morning and he had just awakened. Such a magnificent specimen of humanity he was – so handsome, so well-built, and so confident, standing there as unselfconsciously as any creature of Nature would. I desired him immediately, and I wanted him to desire me.

So I arranged for a tryst with a merman the next morning in full view of Damien's veranda. It went almost too well – Damien dove straight into the ocean and swam to us with powerful strokes, intending to break us apart so he could finish what the merman had begun. But when I realized his intent, I became one with the water. It left all of us frustrated, but the merman lived to love another day.

And Damien was intrigued – so intrigued that when I appeared alone the following morning, he was already in the water. That morning was…

I should not be telling you this.

I should have never let him see what I truly was. I didn't know how ruthless he was, and that once he had lured me into his home, he had no intention of ever letting me go. I became part of his collection, you see. And I was the only Elemental he had.

He learned quickly that he could not keep me prisoner by physical means. He knew I could escape by dissolving because I'd done it at our first meeting. So he moved me from his oceanfront estate to another of his homes, this one in Arizona. There, away from my natural Element, he tried to deprive me of Water, and it nearly killed me.

That would never do. He had to keep me alive. If I were dead, I'd no longer be part of his collection. So thereafter, he kept me prisoner with his words. I was beholden to him for my life, you see. He controlled my access to water but lied to me — he said I could have as much as I wanted, any time I wanted it, as long as I did certain things to please him. But I could never please him enough. I called him cruel, but he told me he was doing this for my own good. He told me my people had rejected me — disowned me — for consorting with a human. I knew that was a lie. I was hundreds of years old and had consorted with mortals before, and had never been rejected by my own kind. Still, I was beaten down enough to believe I would never escape him.

And then I became pregnant with you. I knew immediately that you would be an undine like me. And I knew he could not — *could not* — be allowed to collect you as he had collected me. So I bided my time. And then one glorious day, it rained. Rain! Blessed release! No desert plant was thirstier for rain than I was. I opened my window and wept with joy. And then I let the Water take us away.

I gave birth to you months later, in a bathtub in a rented room, and laughed when you swam out of me head first.

~ ~ ~

"Oh, my dearest child," Mam said, as she crossed the room and pulled me to her. "Don't cry for me. It was a horrible experience, but it was only one, and I have had so many good ones, before and after. And so many of the good ones are due to you."

I dried my tears on her shirt and looked up at her. "He never knew?"

"That I was pregnant? No. He never knew. The monsoon came before I began to show."

"I didn't know why we ran so often," I said. "And then I thought — after you read me the selkie story — I thought you were running to keep him from catching you." I scrubbed at my eyes with my hand, like an overwhelmed toddler. "But yesterday, Gail said he was focused on me. Not you – me." I chuckled humorlessly. "Of course I'd already told him he was my father."

She sucked in a breath. Then she said, "You couldn't have avoided telling him. That's who he is."

"But how did he become so evil?" I asked.

Mam pulled away from me, puzzled. "Evil?"

I nodded. "Shenandoah said he's the ancient evil that has awakened."

Her mouth dropped open. As if in a daze, she resumed her seat on the sofa and pulled the pillow against her torso again.

"This is bad, isn't it?" I said.

"It's bad," she confirmed. "It's very bad indeed."

After another moment, I said, "So... he wasn't possessed by this ancient evil when you knew him before."

She shook her head. "No. He was just your garden-variety sociopathic narcissist. If Shenandoah..." She shook her head again. "Something must have happened."

"Indeed," I said, but inside I was throwing a party. My father wasn't The Terrible Ancient Evil, after all. Not that being fathered by a sociopath was anything to be thrilled about – but it sure beat the alternative.

"Can he be saved?"

My head whipped around. There was Collum, leaning against the kitchen doorway with his arms folded. His gaze was just as guarded.

I forgot to tell you he was here. Tiger punctuated the statement with a yawn.

"How much of that did you hear?" I asked.

He pushed himself upright. "Pretty much all of it. I was in Conor's bedroom, sorting through some of his stuff, when you came in."

"That sounds like grim work," I said, and patted the seat next to me.

"Not nearly as grim as the tale I just heard." He sat next to me and took my hand. "I'm sorry for everything you went through, Ondine. But I have to say I'm glad in one sense."

She smiled. "Because of Raney."

He grinned at her and looked at our intertwined fingers. I caressed the back of his hand with my thumb.

"So. Can he be saved?" Mam asked, repeating Collum's question.

"That, I don't know. It depends on the nature of the entity that has possessed him."

He looked at me. "Do you want to try?"

I blew out a breath, taken aback with the audacity of the proposal. "I... Let me think about that. I've only met him once."

"But he's your father," he said.

"But he was a sociopath to start with. If we do manage to rescue him, we might end up regretting it."

"True," he said. "We can revisit the question later."

"Sounds fair."

We sat quietly for a moment. Then Mam asked, "So Collum, what are your plans now?"

He relaxed against the back of the loveseat. "Well, it appears I'm unemployed." He smiled ruefully. "I have to confess, I checked the wards out of habit last night and everything was fine. Better than fine, actually. I was always just a caretaker. Dunno what Da was thinking, putting me in charge for eternity the way he did."

"You could ask him," I said, inspired.

"Like call him on the phone or something?"

"No. Go and visit him." I squeezed his hand.

Collum's eyes widened. "I could, couldn't I?" Then he winked at me. "As it happens, I've been summoned. Cloch took it upon himself to track down my father to give him a piece of his mind, and he kind of let it slip about Conor."

I stared at him. "You never told them?"

"I've been busy," he said defensively. Then he looked down, shrugging. "To be honest, I couldn't figure out how. I knew Mam would be devastated, and I didn't want to be the one who did that to her." He paused. "So anyway, I was kind of glad Cloch did it for me."

"Well, I'm glad you're going to Ireland," I said, squeezing his hand again. "Family should be together at a time like this."

He nodded. "I'm sure they'll want some of Conor's things. This way I can deliver them in person. And I do miss the place. Once you've been there, it gets under your skin." He looked around. "But I can't stay for long. I also need to clean out this house so I can put it on the market."

"You're not at all interested in keeping the place? Maybe moving here yourself?"

"Nah. The old place is home." He played with my fingers. "I don't know if you can understand that – I know you two moved around a lot. But when Cloch said that thing about how he *is* the land – well, when I heard it, my gut dropped about a foot. I knew he was right because as an Earth Elemental, I'm also the land. *This* land." He pointed at the floor.

"And yet you're going to sell this house," I said archly.

"Well, not this patch of ground specifically," he amended. Raising his voice, he went on, "But yes, I'm selling this house and Tiger is going to have to come home with me."

A streak of orange fur landed in my lap. *Nope. I'm going with her.*

I laughed. "With me? Why?"

I like you. You bring me tuna. And you're not a jerk, like some people. The cat settled down on her haunches and glared at Collum, who rolled his eyes.

"What is the deal with you two?" I asked, petting Tiger absently.

"It's stupid," he said.

It is not stupid.

"It is too stupid, and I can't believe you've held this grudge for so long."

It's not a grudge.

"All right. Sure. It's not a grudge. Whatever, cat."

You see how he treats me? She looked at me with her large, liquid eyes. Then she blinked slowly. *Besides, I like you.*

157

"You mentioned that," I said. "And I like you, too. But I also like Collum, and I want you to make a better effort at getting along." I looked at him. "*Both* of you."

"Yes, ma'am," Collum said with a salute.

Tiger closed her eyes. "I'll take that as a yes," I said, and resumed petting her.

"So what are *you* gonna do next?" Collum asked me.

"Well, I can't finish my hike now. Allen Owings posted the photos he took yesterday at Lost Falls to Instagram." My mouth twisted. "Every paparazzi within a thousand miles of Harpers Ferry will be here by tomorrow, trying to get a shot of me. They'd just follow me onto the A.T. and someone would end up getting hurt. Oh. Whoops." I let go of Collum's hand and fished out my phone. "I was supposed to call Sid back and never did. Hang on a sec."

Collum started to get up. "I should get back at it."

I grabbed his arm. "No, please stay. This won't take but a minute." I hit redial and waited. "Hey, Sid," I said when he answered. "Sorry it took me so long to call you back."

"It's okay," he said. "Things have changed in the interim anyway." He sounded funny. Defeated, almost.

"What things, specifically?" I asked.

"Well." He paused. "I've spent the last twenty minutes on the phone with Dirk."

That didn't sound good. Dirk was the head of the production company for our show. "And?"

"He's a little torqued. You know he bent over backward to accommodate you when you said you needed to take time off. A lot of people juggled their schedules so you could get away from it all. 'Get your head together' – isn't that how you phrased it?"

This was starting to sound like a guilt trip. "Get to the point, Sid," I snapped.

"The point is, you're gone."

"What?"

"When they saw those photos online, they decided they'd been had. Time is money, Raney."

I was shocked. "But what about the rest of this season? There's only, what, two more weeks of shooting left? I'm free now. I can catch a flight from D.C. and be there tomorrow. That's way sooner than I originally promised to be back."

"Sorry, honey. They've already hired someone else to do the rest of this season."

"Who?" I asked instantly.

"He didn't tell me. The point is they think you're a liability now. They've moved on. I suggest you do the same."

"That sounds like you're firing me," I said faintly.

Sid sighed. "I'm sorry, honey, but this isn't the first time you've flaked on a project I lined up for you. I have my own rep in this town to think of."

"I didn't flake!" I said. "I was stuck in Hawaii! There was a typhoon! All the flights to the mainland were canceled!"

"That's not how the money men see it," he said. "I'm sorry, Raney. I wish you all the best, truly. I'll make sure they send you your final check on time, and that all your stuff from your trailer gets sent to your house."

"Thanks, Sid," I said. "Talk to you later, I guess." I ended the call and shoved the phone back in the pocket of my shorts.

"You got fired?" Collum said. "Why?"

"The producer saw the photos online and he thinks I lied about needing time away." I shook my head. "I bet he thinks I was two-timing him with another project. There have been a bunch of rumors that we wouldn't be optioned for next season. He probably thinks I found another job and was about to cut *him* loose."

"Wait. What photos?"

"There's a spread in the *Sentinel* this morning," I said tiredly. "Allen Owings uploaded the story to Instagram."

159

"Oh, boy," Collum said in dismay.

"I'm so sorry, dearest," Mam said.

Collum wrapped his arms around me, and I leaned against him gratefully. "It's just a shock, that's all," I murmured. "I'll be fine."

I knew I would be, eventually. I just didn't know how long "eventually" would be.

CHAPTER 18 – STILL TUESDAY, THE NEW WORST DAY OF MY LIFE

I spent the rest of the day moping. I felt like I was entitled.

At around four o'clock, Mam said, "Perhaps you should take a bath."

I snorted. "I need more than a bath," I said. "What I'd really like to do is go down to the river, but I'll never get there without being hounded to death. I assume we're surrounded by paparazzi by now."

We are, Tiger said.

"See?" I told Mam. "I've got no way out."

Collum poked his head out of Conor's bedroom. "Did you say you want to go to the river? I can get you there."

"Oh, really?" I said sarcastically. "How?"

"Shortcut," he said with a grin.

Less than thirty minutes later, we were hiking the same section of the A.T. where I'd found Conor's body.

Collum had brought us into the Otherworld through a gate in the back corner of Conor's tool shed, and out through a makeshift gate in the woods near the A.T. "This is how I got to you that day," he said as we stood in a pleasant meadow in the Otherworld, just before he rent the veil between the worlds.

"So you can make a gate anywhere?" I asked, impressed.

"Pretty much, yeah."

"How do you know where to put it?"

"Trial and error. Also, I've done this one before, so there's a bit of an energy signature left. See?" He pointed to a spot in the air.

I thought maybe I saw a little spangle of something, although it could have been dust motes gleaming in the sunlight. I nodded politely.

He cocked his head and set his lips in a line. "You can't see anything, can you?"

I shook my head.

He sighed. "It's okay." Then he drew a silver knife from his pocket, intoned a few words in a language I thought I should understand, and made an L-shaped slash in the air. Then he put the knife away and took my hand. "Let's go." And we stepped through together, from the Otherworld meadow into the forest near the Shenandoah River. The A.T. was just steps away.

As we joined the trail, I said, "We don't have to go back to the same spot where I found Conor. Anywhere along here is fine."

"Up to you," he said. "You're the undine."

A few steps farther along, I said, "You don't have to stay."

He grinned slyly. "And miss seeing you come out of the water again? Not a chance."

I slid my arm around his waist and leaned up to kiss him. Then I sighed. "I'm going to miss you when I go back to L.A."

"I'll miss you, too," he said.

I hugged him again, then began to scout for a spot to enter the river. A few minutes later, I saw a suitable spot upriver from the place where I'd found Conor's body. The bank wasn't too high, so I could get in and out with no trouble, and vegetation sheltered the view of the river from the trail. "Here. This is good," I said, and struck off down the slope with Collum right behind me.

I kept my back to him as I shucked off my clothing. As I folded and stacked my things, I glanced at him and saw the avid look in his eye. "Later," I promised.

"I'm holding you to it," he said.

Then I lowered myself into the river and let go.

The familiar dance began – each droplet of me finding a droplet of river water, partnering, sliding, purifying, restoring. My conflicting emotions over my father, my horror at his treatment of my mother, my concern over my origin story, and the shock of losing my job on top of everything else – all dissolved and floated away downstream. The river took my burdens from me and made me new.

When the goddess's face came into view, I was ready. "Thank you, Shenandoah," I said. "Thank you for healing me."

"It was well deserved," she replied. "You have done us a great service. We are pleased for the opportunity to repay the favor."

"How is Alex Drake?" I asked, since I had the opportunity. It's not that I didn't trust the goddesses' word – I did. But now that my own anguish had eased, I was curious about what they were putting him through.

Laughter bubbled through her response. "Alex Drake is a difficult case. But he will be returned to land by and by, and when that happens, you will find him a more conscientious person than he has been in the past."

Conscientious, huh? I almost wished I could stick around long enough to see it happen.

"There is one more thing you should know," she said.

This sounded serious. "Oh?"

"When Potomac and I came to aid you and the land wight, we pulled significant resources from our usual courses."

I knew they had brought a lot of water to Lost Falls. "How significant?"

"Enough that a portion of Potomac's bed near our confluence was exposed to the air."

If I'd been reassembled, I would have whistled. "That's significant, all right."

"We did not realize it at the time, but a certain sensitive area was uncovered by our actions. A hidden access point."

"Like Collum's gates?"

"Yes, in a way. But this one did not lead to the Otherworld. This one led to a vault."

163

"What's in the vault?"

"Something that was hidden there millennia ago. A key to a lock that must never be opened."

This was starting to sound bad. "Where's the lock?"

"Also hidden."

Naturally. "So the lock is on a door or something, right? What's behind the door?"

"A tool with which the Earth might be destroyed."

"Of course." I thought for a moment. "Why are you telling me this? Did someone break into the vault while the river bed was exposed?"

"Yes."

"Who?" I asked, although I was pretty sure I knew the answer.

"Your father."

If I'd been corporeal, I'd have nodded. "I knew you were going to say that. So I'm going to have to track him down, aren't I? And get this key back from him?"

"We cannot ask you to do this," Shenandoah said. "It is not our place. And it is too much to ask of one undine."

"But if you asked a team of Elementals…" I paused. "That was the real reason for forming the team, I bet. Avenging the death of a gnome is small potatoes, really. What you really want us to do is catch Damien before he destroys the world."

Silence. Then Shenandoah said, "We are not the ones asking this of you."

"Okay, then who's doing the asking?"

"Earth Herself."

I digested that bit of information. "Are the other Elementals getting this same message, or am I supposed to be the messenger? Is Rufus seeing it in his flames or something? Is Gail hearing it on a breeze?"

"You are all being informed separately."

"Well, that's a relief." I pondered this call to action. It wasn't like I had anything else going on at the moment, but still. "I'll talk with the others. We'll let you know what we plan to do."

"We have delivered the message," she said. "That is all we were asked to do."

As she began to withdraw, I said, "Wait. Can I ask you one more thing? Do you know where my father is now?"

"No."

No, of course not. And it should be easy enough to find him. It's not like the planet is huge or anything. "All right. Thank you for answering my questions."

The goddess nodded and withdrew, leaving me feeling like I needed another bath to wash away the emotions stirred up by this one. At least I wasn't upset anymore about losing my job. I'd been sick of the uncertainty about the show's future, anyway.

Replacing it with uncertainty about earth's future wasn't ideal. But it was better than nothing.

I began to pull myself together as I made my way to the bank. The first thing I noticed was two gnomish feet, shoeless, dangling in the water. I ran a finger along the sole of the foot closest to me, and ducked to avoid being kicked.

"Cut that out," he said as I surfaced.

"It's your fault," I said, "leaving temptation in my way like that."

He slid off the bank and into the river next to me. "Speaking of temptation," he said, and swooped me into his arms.

The river bottom was treacherous – covered in stones and other debris – and we slipped more than once. But we managed to fulfill my earlier promise without either of us drowning.

Later, as we got dressed, I said, "So did you get the word about Damien?" I was never going to be able to bring myself to call him Dad. *My father* was the closest I expected I would come.

He nodded. "Yeah."

"What do you think?"

165

"About what?"

I paused in the act of zipping my shorts. "About going after him."

He shrugged. "I've got nothing else going on right now." I shivered at his phrasing, so close to what my own had been. "Besides, I'm already committed to going to Ireland to take Conor's stuff to my parents."

"What does Ireland have to do with it?"

"That's where Damien went," he said. "Didn't Shenandoah tell you?"

"She didn't know." I combed my hair back with my fingers, and then slipped my arms around the waist of my friendly neighborhood gnome. "Care for some company? I've never been to Ireland."

"I was hoping you'd say that," he said as he bent to kiss me.

Author's Note

When I first contemplated writing the *Elemental Keys*, I had been working with mythology for so long that I thought I would need to read a ton of stuff about the Elements and fairies and so on. But I've been reading fantasy for decades, and I guess I've been paying more attention to the Good Neighbors than I thought. However, these books have been useful: *A Complete Guide to Fairies and Magical Beings* by Cassandra Eason; *Fairies* by Morgan Daimler; and *Demons and Spirits of the Land: Ancestral Lore and Practices* by Claude Leconteaux. I also discovered some helpful ways to think about Elemental beings at https://www.whats-your-sign.com/nature-symbols.html.

In the fall of 2018, as I began planning this book for NaNoWriMo, my daughter Kat and I took a day trip to Harpers Ferry to get the lay of the land, so to speak. I'd been there once before, but it had been years. If you have any interest in Civil War history, I'd recommend a visit.

It might sound crazy that a river could be sucked dry, but it actually happened about two years ago – and it wasn't due to magic, either. A huge wind storm created a tidal surge along the New England coast, causing a blowout among tidal bodies of water farther south – including the Potomac River at Washington, DC. For a few hours, the river bottom was laid bare. Seems like that would give somebody just enough time to find and dig up something that ought to have stayed buried – like an Elemental key, perhaps?

Thanks as usual to my editor, Susan Strayer, for catching all the continuity errors I made while finding my feet with this work.

And I'm grateful to all of my readers who have gotten this far. Would you do me a favor, please, and leave a review? I'd appreciate it — and so will the readers you'll be helping to decide whether to give this series a try.

Lynne Cantwell
March 2020

ABOUT THE AUTHOR

Lynne Cantwell writes mostly urban fantasy and paranormal romance, with a dash of magic realism when she's feeling more serious. She is also a contributing author for Indies Unlimited. In a previous life, she was a broadcast journalist who worked at Mutual/NBC Radio News, CNN, and a bunch of other places you have probably never heard of. She has a master's degree in fiction writing from Johns Hopkins University. Currently, she lives near Washington, D.C.

Also by Lynne Cantwell:

The Pipe Woman Chronicles Universe
Seized: Book One of the Pipe Woman Chronicles
Fissured: Book Two of the Pipe Woman Chronicles
Tapped: Book Three of the Pipe Woman Chronicles
Gravid: Book Four of the Pipe Woman Chronicles
Annealed: Book Five of the Pipe Woman Chronicles
The Pipe Woman Chronicles Omnibus

Where Were You When: A Land, Sea, Sky Anthology
Crosswind: Land, Sea, Sky Book 1
Undertow: Land, Sea, Sky Book 2
Scorched Earth: Land, Sea, Sky Book 3
The Land Sea Sky Trilogy

Dragon's Web: Book One of the Pipe Woman's Legacy
Firebird's Snare: Book Two of the Pipe Woman's Legacy
Spider's Lifeline: Book Three of the Pipe Woman's Legacy

Turtle's Weir: Book Four of the Pipe Woman's Legacy

A Billion Gods and Goddesses: The Mythology Behind *The Pipe Woman Chronicles*

The Transcendence Trilogy
Maggie in the Dark: Transcendence Book 1
Maggie on the Cusp: Transcendence Book 2
Maggie at Moonrise: Transcendence Book 3

Stand-Alone Novels
SwanSong
The Maidens' War
Seasons of the Fool
Mom's House: A Memoir

Short Story Collections
Back Home Again: The Five59 Stories, plus a few

Contributor
Indies Unlimited 2012 Flash Fiction Anthology
Indies Unlimited 2013 Flash Fiction Anthology
Indies Unlimited 2014 Flash Fiction Anthology
Indies Unlimited Tutorials and Tools for Prospering in a Digital World
Indies Unlimited Tutorials and Tools for Prospering in a Digital World, Vol. II
13 Bites
Summer Dreams
Boo!: Volume 2
Winter Tales
Plan 559 from Outer Space

Other Realms
13 Bites Vol. III
I Heard It on the Radio
Plan 559 from Outer Space Mk. II
13 Bites Vol. IV
Other Realms Volume II
Plan 559 from Outer Space Mk. III
Free for All: A Writers' Anthology
13 Bites Vol. V
Boo! Volume 5: A Fifth of Boo!

Find Lynne on Teh Intarwebz:

Facebook: http://www.facebook.com/pages/Lynne-Cantwell
Twitter: http://twitter.com/lynnecantwell
Goodreads:
http://www.goodreads.com/author/show/696603.Lynne_Cantwell
Pinterest: http://pinterest.com/lynnecantwell
Ravelry: https://www.ravelry.com/people/lynnecm
Blog: http://www.hearth-myth.com